Shadows Rising

Midnight Guardian Series Book 4

Bryna Butler

ISBN-13: 978-0-9859272-4-0
Swancrest Publishing
Printed in the United States of America.

MIDNIGHT GUARDIAN SERIES

Book 1
Of Sun & Moon

Book 2
Whispering Evil

Book 3
Midnight Child

Book 4
Shadows Rising

Book 5
Book of the Lost
Coming Spring 2013

Book 6
House of Gammen
Coming Late 2013

DEDICATION

This book has been the hardest to write. Structuring problems and consistency issues forced numerous re-writes and delays. I was ready to quit a few times, and when those thoughts crept into my head, I would remember the advice that my father gave me as a child.

Work smarter, not harder
and
A job worth doing is worth doing well

And so, I dedicate this book to him. Thank you for instilling in me the inspiration and work ethic for getting the job done.

For hundreds of years, these dark woods have held a secret. Every living part of it knows the secret, from the top-most leaf on the tallest oak to the tiniest earthworm needling through the earth below. They see them. They hear them. They feel them. They fear them. They are forced to watch, with no way to stop them, no way to scream out.

Oh, I see, you want to know what they're looking for. That's easy. They only want one thing. They're looking for blood, human blood. The shadows latch onto their victims. They roll over the victims face, covering their mouth and nose. It's no use to fight or to gasp for breath. They will continue to hold until their victim loses consciousness. Then, this poor person is dragged across the woodland floor to a hiding place where the shadows leave them to find their next victim. If a victim should regain consciousness while the shadows are away, the unfortunate soul would still find himself lost in the shadows' hiding place deep in the woods, soon to be re-captured by the creatures. There is no hope.

I know this seems like a terrible fate, but you must understand we've only just begun this cautionary tale. For you see, the shadows are just errand boys. It's their master that is the real monster of the story. The shadows only attack during the full moon. The moon's glow gives them form. The shadows hunt and take victim after victim. Once they have collected enough bodies; they call their master, a beast that they have named Emperor.

– *Of Sun & Moon*

A child born of sun and moon will impart a human gift to bring forth the fall of the house of Gammen.

— *Hayes Prophecies*

Prologue

I almost had it. A tiny green vial grazed the tips of my fingers as the ceiling fell in on me. If the drawings on the cave walls were any indication, the vial contained a substance that would open the barrier that separates the human world from the Mogdoc Empire. The mogdocs are wicked little creatures so maybe it's for the best. Maybe it's safer that the vial was destroyed. Maybe it was never meant to be used.

But then again, I'm not really a "maybe" kind of girl.

I'm Keira Ryan, a guardian and the child born of sun and moon. My best friends are a time traveler and a seer, but even they can't help me. They can't see my future. It's all on my shoulders to stop Broo Gammen, the shapeshifting, emotion-controlling girl named empress who is in desperate pursuit of a way to penetrate the barrier and take revenge upon the human world that banished her kind, the mogdocs, from the face of the Earth.

An ancient prophecy hidden away in an old book

says that I'm the key to her downfall. It also says that I need the human gift and that's not panning out so well.

It's been two days since the vial, the answer to it all, slipped from my grasp. Its green glow still haunts me. I see it every time I close my eyes. Every time! The scenario runs over and over in my mind making me feel like a hamster trapped on its wheel. I just can't seem to let it go and for good reason. Little Drew Hayes is being held captive by Empress Gammen and her mogdoc empire. He's a toddler that is destined to one day change the world, and he's my charge, my responsibility.

To make matters worse, the friends that I mentioned before are suffering. The seer and the time traveler, that's Colby and Ann. Empress Gammen's demonstration of strength at prom left Colby on crutches and put Ann in the hospital. Everyone is depending on me to find the gift, and use it to defeat the not only the Empress, but the entire House of Gammen.

The "human gift"…no description. Of course, there would be no description. That would make it all too easy, and my life is anything but easy. Everyone has their own theory; the most popular being that the gift is actually a person. The lineup of suspects includes my charge, my best friend, and even my future baby. I don't even want to talk about that last one.

They're all wrong anyway. I think it's some*thing,* not some*one.* I don't have anything to back that up, just my gut and a little wishful thinking, I guess.

That's what led me to the Great Serpent Mound and to that tiny green vial tucked away underground in a ceremonial mogdoc cave. But here's the thing that's been gnawing at me. According to the prophecy, I'm supposed to impart a *human* gift. That vial and its glowing, magical contents didn't seem human at all. So, follow me on this, I'm thinking that it wasn't the gift. I'm thinking that it was just a means to get the gift...which begs the question. Is there another way?

I shared this thought with my father. That was a dead end. He doesn't buy into my ideas easily. Not that I've seen him lately to discuss it. He's always in Elsted working on a lead of some sort. He likes doing things his way. I take after him in that. Normally I'd say, "Yay, Dad!"

Only this time, his way seems to entail a lot of book research and face time with the guardian elders. Timewasters if you ask me. I already know what I have to do. My life can be summed up in four not-so-easy steps. Find the gift. Rescue the child. Stop the House of Gammen. Save the world.

Only I'm back to square one. Again. If square one was a spot on the globe, I'd be the mayor.

Chapter 1: Eight Moments in Time

Colby Hayes was not the kind of boy that kept secrets.

A responsible guy, he never put off homework. He gladly did his chores. He always ate his vegetables. He never told lies.

Yet, Colby hadn't yet told the others of what he now knew. Broo had given him everything back. She used her power over emotion to unlock his forgotten night of time traveling with Ann. Forgotten wasn't the right word, though. Stolen. Colby's memory of the night was stolen by Broo's brother, Brun Gammen.

On that stolen night, Ann traveled back from the future and essentially kidnapped Colby; snatched him right from the movie theatre concession stand with a kiss and a sonic boom. Why? She couldn't, rather wouldn't, explain. She said it was too dangerous.

They spent the night hopping from one point in time to another. Future Ann called this a "nudge", a push in the right direction. She cautioned him about sharing information. "You nudge one person, not a crowd," she explained. "Anything more than that could cause repercussions of the disastrous variety. Trust me."

Truth be told, he did trust her. She had never given him reason not to. He would take her word for it. After all, *she* was the time traveler. Still, Colby couldn't shake the feeling that he was not unlike Ebenezer Scrooge being shown the past so that he could make the right decisions in the present. Yet, another thought pulled at his brain. Why me?

Colby searched his memories of that night. He needed answers. They were somewhere in eight moments spread throughout time.

ONE

Ancient Greece, Athens, Exact Year Unknown

The damp night air hinted at spring. Roses surrounded them, giving off their strong perfume which forced Colby's nose to run and eyes to water. He sneezed. Ann shushed him and pulled him behind a large bush of yellows. Her tiny fingers parted the leaves, careful not to touch the thorns. From their hiding place they spotted a girl swinging her legs as she sat on a stone bench a short distance away. Her simple white tunic fluttered gently in the warm breeze, but she paid it no mind. The girl flung a single rose to the ground. Her tear-streamed eyes were focused on her index finger.

Ann prodded Colby with her elbow. He turned to see her pointing to another young creature making its way through the garden entrance and down the path toward the bench. Colby's mouth dropped open. He had never seen one before. It appeared to be a mogdoc *child.*

Its claws, though tiny, still looked lethal. Its skin, a shade of blue-green and scaly like any other mogdoc, seemed more vibrant, more iridescent, than the ones he had seen prior. Oddly, the creature seemed happy, almost smiling, skipping and jumping as it made its way down the path. A tiny pouch looped around its neck bounced up and down against its chest.

When the mogdoc child reached the girl on the bench, Colby nearly leapt from his hiding spot. Ann held him back.

"Just watch," she whispered. "We can't interfere."

Distracted by the scene before them, he hadn't realized how close Ann was until she spoke. She seemed oblivious to the closeness as well, her hand remained on his back, urging him to stay down.

The girl was crying, and the mogdoc shushed her gingerly. Crooked, clawed fingers reached out to remove strands of the girl's long brown hair from the path of her tears. It appeared to be consoling the girl. The mogdoc child dipped a claw into the pouch on its chest and spread the contents, what appeared to be some type of primitive medicine, on the girl's finger.

To Colby's amazement, the girl did not run or scream. She sat quietly while the mogdoc rubbed the medicine onto the spot where the rose thorn pierced her skin. After a few moments, the girl wiped the tears from her face and hugged, actually hugged, the mogdoc. The kids, hand in hand, then skipped into a nearby building.

"How can a mogdoc and a human be friends?" Colby asked.

"This was before," Ann said, her eyes pleading with him to understand. "Three days from now, the mogdoc will eat the human girl. This story will be told over and over again by the guardians as a warning. Even the youngest mogdoc is manipulative and evil beyond all imagining."

Her words stirred a memory in him. "I know this story, don't I? The mogdoc befriended the girl to gain access, played tea party to sweeten the blood, and healed her… Whoa, that just happened. The mogdoc healed her from the rose thorn to save every drop of blood until the time was right."

"Yes," she agreed. "Keira told you this story on the day she gave you your Atlantis token."

"How could you know that?"

"One day very soon you will tell me," she smiled and brushed his bangs from his frightened eyes. "And I will hang on your every word."

He squinted at her, but she didn't bother to explain the comment. Distracted by a stray thought, she pulled her hand away and moved on.

"I thought it might be helpful to see this. Hearing is one thing, but seeing it with your own eyes is quite another. See how believable the mogdocs can be?"

"I know what you mean. It seemed to genuinely care about the girl."

"Maybe it did."

"Yeah, right," Colby said.

"I mean it. Mogdocs are creatures rooted in evil. For them, love is desire and obsession. It's messy. Don't forget that," she said a bit shortly. "That's enough of this one. We have plenty more stops to make before the night is over."

TWO

Gammen Residence, outside of Dallas, Texas
15 Years Ago

The mesquite bush scratched Colby's arm when they appeared practically on top of it. He clamped his hand over the abrasion.

Ann hadn't noticed. She pushed him down quickly so that they would not be detected. The two then inched up, just high to see inside the window. The room looked a bit dated, but was otherwise a perfectly normal family living room.

"Father! Father!" a little girl shouted. Her bright, blond curls sprang to life as she bounced with delight, highlighted by an eerie, unnatural light.

Colby turned to see if a car was approaching. The bush would not provide adequate cover. There was no car. Not in the driveway. Not even on the road. All was quiet and still.

He didn't look away until Ann touched his shoulder. "Let me see," she whispered, pointing to where he still clutched the scratch on his arm. "Oh, for cryin' out loud! We'll have to stay outside now. He'll definitely smell you if we try to hide and watch from inside. We can't take that chance."

"Who'll smell m…" Colby started to ask, but the answer appeared in the window before them. The man brought his other foot through the source of the odd light. It was a mogdoc threshold, right in the middle of the living room. The man stepped across the mogdoc threshold and it sealed itself so that it was little more than a seam of light hanging in the air. Hidden beneath a long, dark hooded robe, he stood tall in the center of the room. Ceremonial beads hung down one side. This robe was very similar to the last one Colby had seen him wear. It was the last one anyone had seen him wear.

"Princess," he exclaimed. "Oh, how I've missed you." He scooped up the girl and spun her around in the air.

Colby had to remind himself to breathe as the little girl with gorgeous green eyes giggled. She flung her arms in the air as if flying, completely trusting the evil ruler of the mogdocs. "Brooke," Colby's whisper trembled.

"Broo," Ann corrected. "Bov and Broo. Alexa is there in the corner and…"

Colby directed his eyes over to a worn recliner in the corner of the room where a wearied young mother sat with her son on her lap. The mother edged out a meager smile at the sight of her husband. The boy nestled into her chest. With hair as black as the Atlantean sky, Ann didn't have to finish her sentence. Colby knew that the boy had to be Brun.

"Princess," Bov said, setting the girl down. "I have a present for you and your brother."

"Is it a nanny?" Alexa asked, her voice haggard.

He strode to her, his presence such a force that the mere action of walking was a thing of intimidation. With a small squeak, Brun hopped from her lap and ran to his sister. Bov leaned over Alexa, trapping her in her chair.

"Raising my legacy is the highest honor conceivable. Surely you are not suggesting that you wish to give that up. What use would you, a mere human, serve to the Empire then?"

She slid out of the seat and to her knees. "It is my honor to raise *our* children," she replied, her nose nearly touching his feet.

Satisfied by her display of obedience, Bov moved back to the center of the room again turning his attention to the children. The girl excitedly bounced in the air in anticipation of the promised gift; while the boy stood quietly, shyly beside her. Bov's eyes covered the boy before he let out a conspicuously heavy sigh of frustration.

"My offspring, today is the first step in your rise to power."

Alexa cocked a brow, now clearly more interested than before. She delicately moved back to her seat. Ann prodded Colby toward the children. She didn't want him to miss it.

Emperor Gammen now knelt before the boy and the girl. Their eyes, the same mogdoc green as his, matched his gaze as he lifted a copper coin in front of them.

"Pretty," the girl laughed. The boy cautiously reached for it.

"Ah, ah, ah," Bov cautioned.

Before them, he waved his empty hand over the coin and then there were two. The little girl was amazed. She let out a squeal and clapped. Concern wrinkled the little boy's forehead.

"Well that was seriously cheesy," Colby whispered, but Ann quickly stifled him.

"Alexa, we will need privacy. Pull the curtains and disappear."

"Always the gentleman," Colby muttered under his breath.

"I said to hush. Do you *want* him to find us?"

Colby glared at Ann and mouthed the word "fine" before following behind her. She guided him away from the window just as Alexa stepped toward it and reached up to pull the rusty orange drapes closed.

"Back here," Ann whispered.

"Why?"

Ann didn't favor Colby with a response, but instead pulled him along. He stumbled around the corner of the house. Ann was standing, back against the wall, looking at her silver watch.

"You still have the watch," Colby said. "The one Jump gave you." He realized this Future Ann couldn't be from too far in the future.

"I will never take this watch off," she said, trying a little too hard not to look up. "I didn't remember you being such a chatterbox."

"Well, since I'm talking too much anyway. What are we waiting for?"

"Alexa is going to drive away in twenty, no seventeen seconds. Once the coast is clear, we can head back over to the window. With that cut on your arm, we can't chance going inside. He'll smell the blood. We'll just have to listen from out here. I hope it's good enough."

"Why wait. Just tell me what we're doing here."

"My words aren't enough. You have to witness what they went through."

"Bov?"

She shook her head and the corners of her mouth fell. "We can only watch. You can't try to save them no matter how much you want. This is part of who they are."

"He HURTS them? His own children. Brooke. No, Ann. No, I do not want to see that."

A bloodcurdling squeal broke into their conversation. "No, Father! No! No! No!" the boy screamed.

Ann grabbed Colby's hand and sprinted back to the window. Alexa had tugged the curtain a little too hard, leaving a tiny hole where the curtain didn't meet the bottom corner of the window. Ann pushed Colby's head to it.

Bov had hold of the child in an iron-clad grasp with a single hand. The boy tried in vain to pull away from his father. Tears tumbled down his cheeks. "I don't want it. I don't want it," the boy cried.

"Coward!" was the word that flew from Bov's lips like a whip. "You weak thing, how are you a son of mine? They will rip off your head the second you ascend to my throne."

The Emperor's mogdoc claws eased from beneath the long sleeves of his cloak and drew a line inside the boy's elbow. Brun's scream pierced a new octave and reached into the rafters.

"Baby," Bov guffawed. "Your sister even laughs at you."

Broo stood off to the side, her beautiful eyes wide. Bov was wrong. She wasn't laughing, but she wasn't helping either. When Bov looked to her, she managed a tight grin which disappeared the second he looked away.

Bov smeared the thin line of blood as he slipped one of the smashed coins, an Atlantis token, into the boy's arm.

"Human with a token," Bov sneered. "We will beat the rats at their own game."

"I not human," the little boy cried.

Gammen responded with a backhand to the boy's cheek. It reddened in an instant which made the Emperor smile.

"Do you think you are mogdoc?" he laughed. "Do you think you are royalty? You disgust me. You will never be anything but a sniveling beast. You shame us all."

The boy, Brun Gammen, collapsed onto the floor. His body lay still and eerily quiet. Tears ran down his stinging cheek, but he no longer sobbed. Colby could see it in his face. This must have been the thing that Ann wanted him to see for himself. The boy was broken.

"Are you ready? Now it is your turn, my Princess," Bov turned to Broo.

Colby clenched his fists. Ann took a step back from him.

The girl lifted her chin and paraded into her waiting father's arms. A sinister smile played across his thin lips. She thrust her arm out straight, and despite her young age, looked him in the eye. It was a challenge and she was up to it, ready to take the coin.

It was more than Colby could stand. From nothing, a lump formed in his throat. He couldn't swallow. No matter what she had done to him in the past, he couldn't just watch this happen to her. She was only a little girl. She couldn't have been more than six years old. This tiny, brave girl didn't deserve to be mutilated by her father.

His mouth opened as he tried to catch his breath. Broo had controlled him through his emotions on more than one occasion, but she didn't have control of them now. It was him, all him, as he spun around Ann and sprinted for the front door.

The sun-dried grass crunched under each footfall. He heard Ann's pace quickly match his. He had the head start though. He didn't dare look back, fearing that would decimate any tiny lead he had over her.

Colby felt a hand brush his back, but it wasn't enough to bring him to a halt. He leapt to the top step and put a hand on the doorknob.

Ann tackled him sideways. His left cheek slammed onto the concrete porch as she crashed on top of him.

"What did I say?" Ann whispered, between the deep gasps for air. "What are you thinking? You can't go in there. We can't interfere. We can't be seen."

"I can't let him hurt her. She's just a little girl. What if we save her? Then maybe…"

"She's going to become Empress, whether you save her or not."

"You don't know that."

"I know that when you interfere in the timeline, things go bad," Ann said as she let go and leaned back. "This was a mistake. I should have never brought you here. It's all going wrong again."

"What do you mean again?"

She clenched her teeth and shook her head. "Not you. Something else. I tried to change something else and it just got worse and worse, until you…" Her eyes glistened as she looked away from him.

"I'm not going to pretend to know what you are talking about, but this is different. I'm trying to save her life."

They heard a rustling inside the door. Ann's eyes pleaded with him and she mouthed, "She'll be fine. This doesn't kill her."

"Whatever," he whispered back and ushered her into the bushes just off the porch.

The door didn't open. They stood there together, hidden by an overgrown forsythia spilling over with yellow blooms. He quietly watched and waited. “Thank you,” she looked up to him. He was still angry, returning her sentiment with just a nod, not even as much as a glance her way.

Ann took his hand in hers. “I mean it. I know it’s hard to let it all happen and do nothing.”

He let down his guard a little. “Listen, I’m not mad, I just don’t understand why. We can change things, Ann. Really change things.”

“No. You can’t.”

“If we just…”

“Their destination is set. All that we could do is change the path.”

“All that we could do is change the path?” he repeated and Ann’s eyes blew open, she put a hand over her mouth.

“What? What’s wrong?” Colby asked.

Ann started breathing hard and fidgeting with the watch on her wrist.

“Ann, talk to me. Are you okay?”

She nodded. “I just…” she breathed. “We need to keep going.”

“After you,” he said and with that she took his hand and they disappeared.

THREE
Valley View High School
September, Freshman Year

Ann slammed Colby against a tree.

His mind whirled as his head ground into the bark. Eyes not yet adjusted to the darkness, he pushed at her. Ann caught his wrists easily, leaned in close, and whispered.

"Behind me. Careful, don't let them see us."

He squinted and tilted his head to see Ann standing behind herself. The one in the distance was a younger Ann, all smiles. Jumper clasped that girl's hand, and they were talking to another girl on a bench. They were just outside the school. Colby stared at them. He would know the girl on the bench anywhere, even if her hair was longer, and he couldn't see her face.

And then, the locker room door opened.

A smile played across Brun Gammen's lips as he approached Keira. The other Ann and Jumper waved goodbye and headed down the sidewalk. Future Ann buried her face in Colby's chest as they passed. Colby tilted his head down to hers, leaving only his forehead and eyes visible.

"Why did you bring me here?" Colby's voice tensed as he spoke.

Ann touched his chin and pulled her head up to face him. Her eyes wet, she only asked him not to interfere. "Just watch," she said.

And he did, although it turned his stomach to do so.

He watched as Keira and Brun laughed and

walked hand in hand.

"What's the point in this?" was what Colby was going to say, but Ann cut him off. She pointed to the couple, but kept her eyes on him.

"3...2...1..."

An autumn breeze captured Brun's ball cap and carried it up into the air. Keira caught it and plucked it back on his head. Her movement so quick, he didn't even have enough time to react. It lasted only a second, or maybe milliseconds, but it was enough to give anyone watching a peek at her true nature. And that's when Colby saw it.

“And you’re quick,” Brun said. Colby noticed a hint of suspicion behind the guy’s words and a bounty in what he had left unsaid.

Keira shrugged and looked away from the boy. It struck Colby as a flirty move; odd on Keira, like a cat in socks. However, it was Brun that commanded his attention. Brun's demeanor had changed. His plastered smile was gone. Colby stayed glued as Brun run his fingers across Keira's cheek and lifted her chin.

And what the mogdoc prince said next should have put a sparkle his green eyes, but instead they reflected pain for he knew what may come of it if his suspicions were validated. Brun’s brow furrowed and his words came strained, but true. “This feels right.”

Colby gasped.

"Then you know why I brought you here?" Ann whispered in Colby's ear.

"Yeah," Colby was breathless. A sick twinge flexed in his chest as he told the ground, “It's the moment he started to fall for her."

FOUR

Keira's House, May, Freshman Year

Soft nothings fell on Colby's head as his knees gave out. In a desperate attempt to slow his fall, he grabbed at whatever he could, but none of it supported him.

Ann reached down, a finger over her mouth. "Shhh," slipped from her pursed lips.

He took her arm silently, though he could barely see it. They were in a room, small and dark. As he touched the walls, rising until he banged his head on the horizontal metal bar, he slowly realized that it wasn't a room at all.

Ann pointed to her eyes, then to the crack in the closet door. Colby pressed his face against it. The room outside waited, lit only by the twilight sun streaming in from the window. Someone waited there, seated on the edge of Keira's bed.

The bedroom door shut lightly. Colby couldn't see who was there as the crack in the door only permitted a partial view of the scene before him. Still, he didn't have to see to feel her presence, to know that it was Keira.

"I wish you no harm," the waiting man said, and when he rose and stepped into the window's light everyone could see that it was Brun.

Colby laughed silently imagining Keira's reaction, punctuated by Brun suddenly raising his hands over his head like a thief surrendering to the police. The prince was charming; however, not charming enough. Colby found himself feeling prouder and prouder of his friend as she brushed off the boy's attempts to sway her, to explain his side.

"Is that what you think?" Brun asked in pure, unaltered exasperation. "You were always so protective of him…"

Colby shot Ann a bewildered look. Brun had only discovered that Drew was Keira's charge recently. This was much earlier than that. This was wrong.

"How does he know about Drew?" Colby mouthed.

To which Ann quickly put a hand over his mouth so that he would hear the rest.

"…The day the police took him, you pushed me. You were so strong, that's when it all clicked."

The police never…ahhhh, Colby realized. The police never took Drew. It was Colby that they took to the police station for questioning their freshman year.

He knew that the Sect and the Unionists had both at one time or another suspected that he was Keira's charge, but it had never occurred to him that Brun was included in that group. However unsettling that was, it was immediately trumped by Brun's next admission. It was an admission of love to which Keira responded with a fire so intense that Colby, still hiding in the closet, found himself taking a step back.

And it went on like that for quite some time. Keira was all fury and Brun was careful confidence. She would ask questions and he would answer and she wouldn't like the answer so she would strike with a threat. And when Keira had had her fill of his grand romantic pretenses, she raised her dagger. In the next second Brun swept behind her and Colby found himself up against the closet door, Ann's hand firmly wrapped around his forearm.

"No," she pleaded silently.

"Just try me, mogdoc," they heard Keira sneer.

The sun's last beams had faded and the room was now dark. Colby squinted through the crack in the door. He couldn't see anything. He turned to say something to Ann, but when her face came into view, he froze.

"Make no mistake; I will not let you forget. You are mine."

The mogdoc prince said the words, but Ann mouthed them in perfect synchronization.

Colby looked to her in disbelief. It was a moment before she realized he was watching. When she did, her mouth opened slightly. She then closed it tightly, wrapped her fingers around Colby's hand, and they disappeared.

FIVE

Outside Harlington Pass, August, Sophomore Year

A rush of nausea cleared to a pounding headache. Colby suspected that his vision was blurred as well; although he couldn't be sure as it was nighttime in the darkened alley. When he arrived, unsteady on his feet, he immediately sunk to a crouch. Ann lowered herself beside him, both hidden behind a dumpster. That didn't help. A rancid stench seeped from its insides and enveloped them.

Colby grabbed onto it, without a thought of how hard he would have to scrub his hands afterward. No, the only thing going through his mind was his urgent need for fresh air.

The dumpster creaked. Ann let out a slight gasp, and yanked Colby back down. She placed a hand over his mouth as he heard a footstep. Then another.

“Insane killer, come out, come out wherever you are," Keira's voice rang out in a cocky sing-song.

Colby and Ann held their breath. The footsteps stopped in front of the dumpster. The lid creaked open slowly, and after a moment she let it go with a thud that echoed through the alley.

As Keira's footsteps trailed off, Ann put a hand on Colby's chest. "Now, you follow," she whispered. "Stick close to the wall. Don't be seen. Don't interfere."

"What about you?"

"Not this one. I...I can't," she said. "When the other You arrives, come back to me and we'll go. And Colby, don't blink."

A rush of air swept past their hiding space behind the dumpster.

"Hurry! Now!" Ann pushed Colby away. He clumsily ran down the alley, stopped short of the end, and ducked into a doorway where he could watch concealed in darkness.

Jumper jogged into view and slowed as he neared the alley. He didn't even see the man in the shadows approach. No, Jumper didn't know the stranger was there until he felt cold steel slide into his back. The attacker didn't bother pulling the knife out. Instead, he shoved Jumper off with supernatural force, sending the boy sprawling through the air. The entire attack happened in the span of seconds. If Colby hadn't heeded Ann's warning--don't blink--he would have missed it.

"Yaahhggg!" pain seared Jumper's voice as he flailed.

His attacker took one human step into the light. Then, with the speed of his father, he caught a nearby fire escape and pulled his body onto it. It was a perfect position to watch what would come next.

The wait was only as long as a heartbeat. Jumper fell onto Keira. Startled by Jumper's yell and impaired by the dark night, her training kicked in, and she reacted as if a mogdoc had pounced on her. Keira grabbed him up by the neck, his feet dangled. Colby wanted to yell out, but even if he could intervene, he wouldn't. He was frozen where he stood by the predatory look in Keira's eyes.

Then something else flashed in them…recognition. Her hands opened and flew off of Jumper, but it was too late. His dead weight slumped to the ground. Keira hovered over the boy, shaking and helpless in her own tears.

Colby knew that Keira still blamed herself for

this. She had even confided in Colby that somehow she had stabbed Jumper on that night. She was wrong.

Brun Gammen lowered himself from the fire escape soundlessly and eased down to Jumper's body.

"He's okay," Colby heard him say.

"William? It…it was an accident. I thought…"

"I know."

Brun's hands checked for a pulse as the two continued to speak in hushed tones. When Colby thought that he couldn't stand to watch anymore, Brun put his arms around Keira and held her tightly. She didn't pull away, but instead buried her tear-stained face in his chest. Rage pushed Colby from his hiding place.

Colby strode just beyond the shadow of the alley and when he came into the moonlight he stopped abruptly, snapping out of it as if it were all a bad dream. He didn't know how he had gotten that far without thinking. He knew he couldn't interfere; Ann had warned him, not once, but many times.

Only Brun faced Colby's direction with Keira still in his embrace. Maybe there was time to step back under the cover of the buildings before anyone noticed him. He took a tentative step backward.

"I know that you won't be with me as long as you have promised your heart to him," Brun looked straight at Colby. The left corner of his mouth turned up as he continued to whisper in her ear. "But Keira, promises…they can always be broken."

Colby didn't even realize his fists were clenched until he felt Ann's hands smooth over them.

SIX

Community Park, September, Sophomore Year

Colby's knees gave and tumbled onto the grass. His head swam as he rolled to a sitting position, and Ann sat down beside him.

"Are you feeling okay?" she asked.

Colby shrugged it off. He couldn't let Ann see that each trip took a greater toll on his body. "Are we home?" he asked, thinking that he could finally put this night behind him.

"Sorry, no, we're in the park, near the pond. This would be a little over a year ago for you."

"How many years for you?"

"Nice try," she smiled. He thought it was a nice smile. At the very least it was a welcome change. At their last stop, she acted so oddly. She knew what had happened to Jumper. She knew that Jump left that night still breathing, only a little worse for the wear. Colby couldn't understand why it bothered her so badly and it clearly did.

He wished he could let it go. He really did.

"What happened back there?"

With that, her smile disintegrated. Ann turned toward him, but looked at her wringing hands instead of his blue eyes.

"Okay, well, I'm just trying to get by with telling you as little as possible. I think that's best."

He didn't nod or make a move. She seemed like a frightened bird. He wouldn't give her reason to take flight. Instead, he waited patiently until she continued.

"It's not that I don't *want* to tell you. I'm just afraid that I'm going to cross that invisible line, and we're all going to pay with bad time juju."

"Bad time juju?" he chortled.

"You know what I mean," she said, waving the comment away. "We can't change things. I was thinking that maybe I shouldn't have come at all–that I shouldn't have tried this, but now I think that was wrong."

"How so?"

"I think we were meant to do this. I can't tell you why, but the pieces are starting to fit. I think this, this trip, is part of what was supposed to happen."

"And you still don't think that I should have barged through the door and carried little Brooke out of that house?"

"Broo," she corrected. "And yes. I still think it was best not to interfere. But this nudge that I'm giving you. It feels right, so let's keep at it."

"And I shouldn't have knocked Brun to the pavement back there? Are you sure? Cause we could always go back and…"

Her mouth twitched up in that nice smile that caused him to smile too.

"Right, so, it's sophomore year, and we're in the park. What are we looking for this time?" he asked.

From the position of the sun, it appeared to be late afternoon. The heat of it pressed on them. A lost bead of sweat tumbled down the side of Colby's face. He unbuttoned his cuffs and rolled his sleeves up.

"Actually, I'm surprised you haven't noticed your buddy already," Ann pointed toward the pond.

Colby followed her finger to an older boy standing near the pond in the shade of a large oak. His shirtless back was to them, he looked as if he was readying himself to jump in. His arms came up to shoulder level, then folded and pushed the air in front of him.

“What’s he doing? Is that tae chi?” Colby asked.

“Look at the ground.”

A layer of black undulated at the boy’s feet. Colby was mistaken in thinking that the shadows were cast by the tree. The black pieces tumbled over each other, rising and falling with the boy’s hand movements. These were the shadows of the guardian bedtime stories, the creatures of night that hunted human forests on the Emperor’s behalf.

The boy turned to the side, and placed a hand flat at his mouth as if he was going to blow a kiss. Colby’s eyes grew. “Brun,” he breathed.

They were too far to hear, but Colby could see his lips moving. Then the shadows began to fade. The boy, Brun, fell to his knees. Frantically, he grabbed at the ground, but only pulled up blades of grass. After several minutes, Colby and Ann watched as the boy gave up. He brushed himself off, ran a hand through his hair, and gazed again into the pond.

“He’s going to try it again. Those were shadows, right? In broad daylight? He’s learning how to control them, just like his Dad. We have to stop him,” Colby said to Ann.

“Don’t worry.”

“Don’t worry! Ann, I can’t believe you are going to just sit here. I…I…”

Ann simply raised a finger to point Colby back to the scene before them.

"Keira? What’s she doing in the park?" Colby asked when he saw his best friend head toward the pond. “She hasn’t wanted to come to the park for years. This doesn't seem like Keira."

"Maybe she doesn’t tell you everything when it

comes to him."

Colby's brow furrowed. His only thought was of Brun and Keira together and it felt like inescapable bugs crawling over every inch of his skin. "I don't think I want to see this then."

Ann rubbed his back. "He doesn't hurt her. Okay? It's just a conversation that I want you to hear."

"Fine," he resigned.

"Just look at me and listen. It would be best to keep our faces turned from them anyway."

Not that Colby heard a word she said. His eyes weren't looking at her. They weren't looking at Keira either. They were locked on the disgustingly perfectly tanned guy in board shorts.

"This whole thing is wrong. He's the enemy. This is what? Just last year. She knew who he was, *what* he was."

"I brought you here to listen. Now hush," she admonished him.

The two listened to the couple by the pond. Colby rolled his eyes as they exchanged pleasantries. Then he heard Brun say, "I've got something for you."

Alarm shot through Colby. Ann grabbed onto his wrist, sure he was about to bolt upright and to Keira's rescue.

"Nothing happens to her, Colby. I promise. Remember? This has already happened."

He knew she was right, but he also knew that Keira had never mentioned the green box that Brun now retrieved from a nearby bench.

Colby was startled again when in a blink, Brun was suddenly behind Keira. He hadn't realized he was holding his breath as Brun brushed Keira's hair aside. The movement came inhumanly quick. Even from that distance, Colby could see Keira flinch too.

He continued to hold his breath until Brun opened the box. A long exhale came when Colby recognized the necklace that Brun placed around Keira's neck. Judging from the look on her face, she recognized it too.

"You recognize the necklace, don't you?" Ann asked.

Colby just nodded, not wanting to voice his response and possibly miss some of Keira's next words.

"Crown jewels?" Keira asked.

"Does it matter?" he heard Brun respond. "You look amazing. Well, it's a bit overkill with the shorts, but you know what I mean. Do you like it?"

"Oh please," Colby grunted, even though Ann was the only one that could hear him. "She's not falling for this."

Keira didn't answer Brun right away. Colby could see that she was carefully weighing her next words. He would have preferred a quick dismissal, but somehow it also reassured him to see her taking her time, making a conscious choice. Maybe she wasn't giving into the mogdoc prince's charms so easily.

And then…payoff.

"William, even if we pretend that this is not stolen, this isn't a present that a friend gives a friend. And that's all we are, just friends," Keira told Brun.

Colby pumped a fist and smiled. Ann chuckled silently at him.

Brun looked uneasy. He tried to convince her to keep the gift, but she waved his attempts away. Finally, she opened the clasp, removed it from her neck, and handed it back to him.

“Anyway, I wanted to see if you found out anything about Arden’s charge,” Keira said.

Colby turned to Ann, confusion plastered his face.

"This is after the mogdocs’ first failed attempt to kidnap Arden’s charge, but before the charge was killed. Keira asked for Brun’s help to figure out why they attacked Arden’s charge."

"She *asked* for his help?”

“And he gave it without hesitation…listen.”

“This is ridiculous,” Colby shook his head, but then Brun unknowingly commanded his attention.

“…to get a taste and still discard her, that’s unheard of,” Brun explained. “Like that night with Jumper, I only smelled it and it took everything I had in me to resist.”

“Jumper Johnson is a charge,” Colby mouthed in sync with Keira. Both came to the same realization at the same point in time, although that time had been altered for Colby. And Colby didn’t need to speak the next thought, because Keira was already voicing it.

“That can’t be right.”

Keira quickly changed the subject; Colby wished she hadn’t. He wanted to hear more about Jumper, but before he knew it Brun was asking for a kiss goodbye.

Colby turned his face to Ann. “Can we go now?”

Ann nodded. “If it matters, she’s not going to kiss him.”

It doesn’t matter, Colby thought. Then, as he faded to the next destination in time, he overheard Keira say, “Colby and I might have plans.” And it did matter.

SEVEN

Outside the Home of Jamie Hayes and family
Last Year, Christmas Day

Ann caught Colby as he started to slide down the icy slope. Coming to his senses, he latched onto her and a nearby tree branch. Using them, he scrambled back up. The limb bounced with his weight, and snow toppled down.

"Don't stand. Sit," Ann instructed. "Be careful. We're on the roof."

She was propped up against the corner where a dormer jutted out from the roof. Colby stretched his legs out in front of him, and wedged a sneaker between the shingles. The cold air held off the nausea rising from his stomach and the pounding in his head. Once stable, he looked around for the first time.

Ann eyed him suspiciously. "You look pale. Are you sure you're alright?"

"Jamie's house?"

"Actually, this is his neighbor's house. Cookie-cutter houses, they all look the same," she shivered.

Colby pulled his sleeves back down, and buttoned them at his wrists. "Tell me we're not staying long."

"Not long. Here he comes now," she pointed toward the next house in the row. Colby recognized it as belonging to his brother, Jamie. He couldn't believe that he had missed the myriad of cheesy Christmas lawn decorations, even the Santa in Bermuda shorts.

Just below them, the air erupted as Brun Gammen stepped from a mogdoc threshold.

"Does everything revolve around him?" Colby asked to which Ann replied, "More than you know."

They watched as Brun walked purposefully around the corner of the garage. A moment later, as if on cue, Keira came running around the house tugging Drew on a bright, red sled behind her.

Colby's forehead wrinkled, but he didn't say a word or make a move. Keira, however, slowed as she noticed tracks in the snow that mysteriously appeared from nowhere.

As Brun revealed himself, Keira's hand moved to her dagger.

"Makes a friend kind of proud to see that she's getting smarter," Ann bumped her shoulder against Colby's.

Colby sighed in agreement, and as he did, a bit of snow slipped from the roof. It gave him an idea.

"As long as we don't do anything that will actually change events, we're okay, right?"

"What are you getting at?" Ann asked.

Colby lifted a brow and grabbed a handful of snow.

Keira did the same. She dropped a few handfuls of snow onto Drew's sled to keep him occupied while she went over to see what Brun was after.

"I know I shouldn't have come," Brun said .

High on the neighboring roof, Colby rolled his eyes and Ann stifled a giggle. He worked his hands over the snow on the shingles, collecting it and packing it tightly before lofting it into the air. It landed at Brun's feet.

Brun jerked his head, eyes steady on Drew. The toddler contentedly tossed the snow that Keira had placed on his sled.

And when Brun said something about Christmas gifts, he pouted and tilted his eyes to the ground shyly.

Again Colby rolled his eyes and sent another snowball into the air. This time, Brun had to brush the bits of ice and snow from his jeans. Accusing eyes flashed to Drew.

Ann thought she should stop Colby, but it was just too much fun. What harm could a little misplaced frozen water do?

Brun certainly wasn't letting their antics stop him. He accelerated the conversation by grabbing onto Keira's hands. "Don't you trust me?" they heard him ask.

"This guy doesn't know when to stop," Colby said, and aimed carefully before sending another snowball Brun's way.

Bullseye! It hit him square in the stomach.

Ann and Colby ducked into the branches covering their small area on the roof; thinking that surely Brun would realize that a toddler couldn't have thrown so precisely and with so much force.

He didn't.

"Cute kid," he said. His eyes searched over the child.

The air left Colby's chest. His fun had unintentionally focused the mogdoc's attention on Drew.

"Better cough up that gift, or I'll have him open fire," Keira played. Brun's eyes moved back to her.

"That a girl," Colby whispered and suddenly he could breathe again…if only for a moment.

Brun presented Keira with a red box. *Bracelet*, he thought. It was about that size. *Does he think he can bribe her?* Keira hesitantly opened it just before another snowball hit Brun.

"Colby Hayes!" Ann protested.

"Slipped?" he shrugged.

"You hit him in the face!"

"Worth it. So worth it," Colby replied.

Keira snapped the box closed. "I'm sooo sorry. I don't understand how he…he's just a baby."

"He's got a pretty good arm for a baby," Brun grumbled.

As the two continued to talk, Ann touched Colby's hand.

"No more. It's time to go. There's one last thing you have to see."

"Do we have to leave so soon? This one's been my favorite by far," Colby noted.

"I bet. Since you missed it, he gave her a knife," Ann said. "Remember that, it's kind of important."

EIGHT

Woods outside the Banes estate, Last Monday

"Colby? What's wrong?" Ann's voice. Frantic. Lost.

His head was too heavy. The ground came fast and hard. A moan rolled out of his lungs as his muscles pulled and pushed at the same time.

Ann. He could hear her, but her words weren't words. They couldn't be. They made no sense. Be that as it may, the sound of her voice entered his ears, like notes in hushed tones, constant and calm. Each one soothed his muscles, until his body became deathly still.

Moments later, a kiss touched his cheek. No. Not a kiss, but blades of grass sprinkled with evening dew. Each one caressed the side of his face as they blew in the light summer breeze. They tickled, those wet little imps, and he pulled away.

"Yes, yes, that's it. Come on, Colby, open your eyes."

"Ann," he said, though it was barely more than a breath as it passed his lips.

"You scared me," she said, as he opened his eyes.

"I think," he said. "I think I wasn't built for time travel."

Her lips let a relieved snicker escape. "Can you sit up?"

He nodded and let her put an arm behind his back to assist. With great trouble, she brought him to his feet. They walked only a few yards, and she helped him to the base of an old oak tree. He already seemed stronger; the color returned to his face.

Ann knelt beside him. She put a hand to his head

as if feeling for fever.

"I'm fine," Colby whispered. "Who are we here to see?"

She temporarily ignored him, and continued to check him over. When she was satisfied, she answered, "your nephew is playing in the woods" and waited for his reaction.

"Drew?"

She nodded and pointed past the oak tree and down the slope. In the bottom, the bright-eyed toddler was picking up rocks and dropping them in a pile. A light giggle rose with each one he dropped.

Colby's smile disappeared as he noticed that the rocks were doing the same…disappearing. He blinked his eyes, thinking it to be a trick of the dark night. It was no trick. Black and smooth like a fog, they settled over the grass just below the child's feet. Colby slid up the tree until he was standing. The bark scraped his back, but he wouldn't have known.

Ann rose with him. Colby knew her eyes were on him. Watching. Waiting. Hoping he wouldn't try to step in. She had already warned him; warned him so many times to only watch, never interfere.

So that's what he did. He was in no condition to outrun her anyway.

He watched as the child continued to throw rocks into the shadow. He watched as more shadows swirled toward the boy. He watched as his nephew cooed and sang, and the shadows danced around him. He even watched as little Drew lifted his tiny hands commanding the shadows to rise around him like an army.

That's when Colby realized why Drew was special; why he received the gift of the vox. And at the edge of the trees, just beyond the reach of the shadows, out of Colby's sight, and under the light of the full moon, Brun Gammen watched the boy and realized it too.

Chapter 2: Mogdoc Social Director

Present Day

Eight secret moments spread throughout time.

"Colby, Colby?"

Eight puzzle pieces.

"Colby?" Keira laughed. "Earth to Colby. You're not having a vision are you?"

"No, sorry, I must have zoned out. Where did you come from?," he asked. He stumbled a little as he moved over the uneven ground of the corn field.

"Guess we had the same idea this morning. What's got you up at this hour?" Keira asked.

"Nothing," he said with an uneasy smile. "It's all in the past."

The sun waited below the horizon as Keira and Colby made their way to The Landing. They hadn't started the journey together. Both troubled by their thoughts couldn't sleep and separately headed for the same sanctuary. It was just one of those things. Coincidence or destiny, who knows? The decrepit shelterhouse at the river's edge was usually a favorite spot to watch the sun set; however, on that day they would watch it rise.

The morning dew left its moisture on the picnic tables of The Landing. Keira didn't let it bother her as she plopped atop the one in the center...her table. Her shoulders bucked at the stiffness of the boards, but finally she settled into a semi-comfortable position and folded her hands over her stomach. The rough wood grazed her cheek as she turned her head to stare out the side of the building at the morning sky.

It was quiet in this place. Keira let the songbirds and the lapping of the river current lull her eyes closed. Colby pushed a windblown hair out of her face before settling into the picnic table's bench seat. He set his crutch on the ground softly so that it wouldn't make a sound.

They didn't need words. They had been friends too long. He could see the frustration on her face. She could see the wariness on his. They sat there together in silence until the sun rose.

And when the strong morning rays finally beamed into the shelterhouse, Colby whispered, "Your Dad will be looking for you."

"He probably will," Keira sighed. "Your parents will be looking for you too."

"I doubt that. The police are coming back this morning with more questions."

Keira rolled to the side to face him. He looked tired and his eyes had lost something.

"How's Jamie holding up?" she asked.

Colby's voice was barely audible as he lowered his head to stare at his feet.

"Honestly, he's not. The police are leaning on him hard. He doesn't have any answers to give them. The doors were locked, and there's no sign of forced entry. Jamie and Mary Sue haven't been ruled out."

“They haven’t been ruled out in their own son’s kidnapping?” Keira sat up, her voice incredulous. "They’re suspects?"

Colby shrugged and didn't answer. He didn't need to. There were no clues to indicate a break-in; to the police that could only mean the kidnapper wasn't a stranger, maybe even family. Was Colby a suspect too? He had been questioned when Bobby Crimson disappeared during their freshman year. Surely that was part of some secret, permanent file somewhere.

"Should you be there for questioning?" Keira pushed.

"I feel like I already am. Can't we just..." he mumbled as he pinched the bridge of his nose in agitation.

She just nodded and lay back down on the table. It was only a few more minutes when Colby was on his feet. Keira sat up. She watched him as he silently paced. She watched his mind work, as she had so many times before. She could practically see the gears turn as he meticulously sorted through the situation.

Yet, she didn’t know what caused the worry in him that morning. She didn’t know Broo had unlocked his memory of a night of time traveling with Ann. She couldn’t know.

Ann had warned him about sharing his experience. A nudge is one person; more than that is interference. Time twists and turns on its own terms. It does not tolerate interference.

"Can you call him?" Colby finally asked.

"Sure," she said and pulled her phone from her pocket. "Who are we calling?"

He put a hand on her phone and lowered it. "William. I need you to call William here."

"That's not a good idea."

"Can you call him? Like you did before? Last Halloween when you yelled for him, he just showed up."

"No, that's not..."

"That's exactly what happened. Can you still do that?" he pleaded.

"I...uh...I don't know. What would you do to him once he showed up?"

"Does it matter?"

"I'm just trying to decide if I'm talking to rational Colby or Broo-controlled Colby or recklessly desperate Colby."

"I'm not joking!"

"And I'm not your mogdoc social director!" she steamed. "If you want him here, you'll have to let me in on your plan."

Colby folded his arms over his chest. He was so very tired of being helpless, of depending on others. He had thought that once, just once…

She shook her head, "It won't work."

He lowered his shoulders in a way that reminded her of when they were five and his step brother told them the Easter Bunny wasn't real.

Colby swallowed hard at Keira's eyes full of pity. He knew more about the situation than anyone. He had been to the future and back and sworn to keep it secret.

He already had the answer. There was so much information, all that he had seen, all that he had yet to sort through. No good would come from roughing up the mogdoc prince. No matter how satisfying that would be. The answer he sought would be in those eight moments.

There was no “goodbye” or even a “see you later” as he stood, crutch under arm, and hobbled away without a word.

Chapter 3: Bedside Manners

Later that morning, Keira shifted in the most uncomfortable recliner on earth. Her eyes were stuck on the white tile floor of Ann's hospital room. The conversation she had with Colby at the Landing still rolled in her head.

Everyone was there. Ann looked better. The color had returned to her face, and she was sitting up in bed on her own. Keira noticed that she kept her bandaged arm covered with the stiff, bleached hospital sheets.

Katie twirled a finger through her hair as she sat on the end of her sister's bed flipping through a celebrity gossip magazine she'd borrowed from the waiting room.

Arden, uncharacteristically wearing all black and with arms crossed over his chest, surveyed Colby and Jumper from his self-imposed sentry position just inside the door.

Colby sat in a hard plastic chair; his left pant leg neatly folded above the cast, a souvenir from prom that started at his upper thigh and continued all the way down and over his foot. He had it propped up on a rail that ran up the side of Ann's bed.

Jumper, in wrinkled cargo shorts and a VVHS football tee, sat beside Colby on the stool he wheeled in from the nurses' station. Jump twirled one of Colby's crutches as the two boys entertained Ann with the story of how they became friends.

"It was the second day of kindergarten at East Valley Elementary," Colby started rather formally.

"The room always smelled like white school glue, construction paper, and Miss Lemon's jasmine perfume," Jumper added. "Ahhh, Miss Lemon."

"I'll take your word for it. I don't recall ever sniffing the teacher," Colby said. "But I do remember Kiki and her lunchbox. She and I were already friends. We knew each other because we were neighbors. We were practically raised together," Colby remembered.

"Who's Kiki?" Katie asked.

Jumper exploded with one of his trademark guffaws.

"That was Keira's nickname when she was little," Ann explained.

"Anyway," Colby continued. "The room was filled with tables and chairs in primary colors. Keira and I were at the red table."

"I was blue," Jumper chimed in.

"Yeah, so when lunchtime came, Miss Lemon told us to get our lunches and go to the door so that we could trek down to the cafeteria. Keira had been bragging all morning that she had a bag of M&Ms

tucked away in her lunch box. It was irresistible. To a kindergartner, candy-coated chocolate is like gold," Colby smiled.

Jumper jumped to his feet, his hands still on Colby's crutch, he thrust it out like a sword. "So I nabbed it."

"You what?" Arden asked, raising a brow.

"Hey, dude, don't judge. She practically laid it out like a challenge. Plus, she made it way too tempting with all that boasting and you know Ryan, she's not exactly a girly girl. Her lunchbox was this blue metal thing. It looked like a boy's lunchbox; so when I picked it up, Miss Lemon didn't even question it."

Keira surrendered a smile, "I got a huge lecture before the first day of school. Nana had warned me about my strength. No showing the other kids what I could do."

Colby and Jumper looked to each other. "That's why you didn't fight for it. I never understood why you were afraid of Jump. I'd never seen you afraid of anyone before," Colby said.

"What's to understand? I'm terribly frightening," Jumper smirked.

"Anyway," Colby resumed with a roll of his eyes. "Keira asked if she could share my lunch. When I asked why; she wouldn't say, but I caught a glimpse of this mean little red-haired kid with her lunchbox."

"So what did you do?" Ann asked Colby, but it was Jumper who answered.

"He marched right up to me. His nose was all scrunched up and his teeth were clenched together. I thought he was going to hit me…or bite me."

"Bite you?" Arden looked shocked.

"Kindergarten, remember," Jumper shrugged. "He looked like a biter. No offense, dude."

"None taken," Colby chuckled.

"Nope, he didn't have to hit or bite. He just yelled at me using that huge noggin' of his. Big, grown-up words sprayed from his mouth like a Gatlin gun. I had never heard a kid talk like that before. By the time he got through with me I was completely intimidated and confused and I just remember holding the lunchbox out to him. He snatched it from my hand, but before he could step away I put a hand on his shoulder."

"And that's when I thought I was done for," Colby chimed in. "I squeezed my eyes shut and waited for the impact."

"But it didn't come."

"No, it didn't come."

They smiled and patted one another on the back.

Ann wiped away tears like it was the most touching story ever told. "I wish I was in your class that first year," she said.

Katie shook her head, "Is that it? There's got to be more."

"Not much," Jumper replied. "I just told him that he had to teach me how to do that. He thought it was funny. The next day, he brought me my own pack of M&Ms, and we've been buds ever since."

"True story," Colby added.

"You mean lame story," Katie grumbled as she moved back to her borrowed magazine.

"I thought that it was a very cool story," Ann encouraged them. "You know, that seems like a very good way to deal with a bully. You can't just sit down and take it and let it fester. That only makes things worse. You just have to suck it up, charge in and hope for the best."

"What did you say?" Keira asked.

"I liked their story."

"Not that, the thing about dealing with bullies quickly instead of waiting around."

"Oh no, Keira, your deal is worlds different, literally," Ann repeated.

"Bullies are universal," Keira said as she stood up and began to pace.

"What are you thinking?" Arden asked hesitantly.

Keira stopped right in front of him.

"I'm thinking that now there's someone new to stand up against."

"Yeah, someday," Ann whispered.

"Why someday? I say we do it now."

Up until that moment, Keira had been fairly silent. Her sudden declaration took everyone by surprise. Arden unfolded his arms and pushed out from the wall. Ann sat up in her hospital bed. Katie closed her magazine. Everyone looked to Keira for a cue of what to do or say next. After a few thoughtful moments, she continued.

"What are we doing here? What are we waiting for?"

"Keira, be practical about this," Arden said. "We don't even know where Drew is. Give the Council time to gather intelligence."

She stepped to the foot of Ann's bed. Ann had been the one in the hospital, but the days had taken a toll on Keira too.

Bags appeared grimly under her eyes. Her fingernails were bitten down; clothing and hair disheveled. Guilt racked her body and soul. The girl who stood before them was only a shell of her former self.

She had barely slept, but a passion filled her now and pushed the right words from her lips. She pulled back her shoulders and stood tall.

“Follow me on this. When we thought Brooke had been taken by the mogdocs, we gathered up our weapons and we went after Gammen. Not days or weeks later, but hours later. Now they have their hands on a helpless child. A child who’s destined to bring us something better. A child whom I have vowed to protect with my life.

“I have to make a stand, but here’s the thing, I can’t do it without you. We are strong together. I know because they keep trying to separate us. They’ve tried to break us apart and still we’re here. No one can stop us. Not the Unionists, not the Sect, not the Empress, not…” she threw Arden a look. “Not even the Prince.”

Arden shook his head. “If we get caught, the mogdocs won’t show mercy. You can’t ask this of your friends. They’re just kids.”

“Who are you callin’ a kid?” Jumper broke in.

Keira put her hands on Jumper’s shoulders and looked him in the eyes.

“He’s right,” she said to everyone’s surprise.

She dropped her hands and turned to the rest of her friends.

“I understand if you want to walk away. It’s the smart thing to do. There’s no shame in it. This isn’t a game. There are no time-outs, and I can’t guarantee your safety. So, dig deep, the decision can only be yours and yours alone.

“This morning, my best friend told me to do

something, and I didn't because my father and the elders say we wait. Well, he was right and I'm the child of sun and moon and I say we fight starting at the Empress's front door. We rescue Drew and stand up against injustice. Who will stand with me?"

Colby took his crutch from Jumper and rose onto his good leg. Everyone watched as he carefully hopped to Keira; the hollow, springy tap of his crutch, the only sound in the room. Each hop-step made precise and deliberately slow.

They waited silently, breaths held, until he reached her.

Colby stopped in front of Keira, less than an arm's length away. He studied his friend in careful consideration of the situation.

He knew what she was trying to pull off–confidence. Yet, her wrinkled forehead and tense jaw gave her away. They gave her away only to him.

"Always," he forcefully declared. He raised the crutch above his head and repeated the word, this time screaming it as an impromptu battle cry, "Always!"

"Always," Ann echoed, the tears returning to her eyes and tumbling down her cheeks, her bandaged left arm raised above her head.

"Yes! I am *so* in," Jumper yelled. "It's about time I get included in the butt-kicking around here."

"Well if he's going to do it, then I am too," said Katie with an indignant lift of her chin.

"How 'bout it?" Keira turned toward her mentor.

"It's completely daft," Arden said with a shake of his head.

"We'll have a plan."

"It won't be enough."

"Maybe not, but at least we will have tried. You

once told me that I was supposed to be the greatest guardian to ever live. I see that now is the time to do something great. Will you help me? Will you stand with us?"

Arden looked into every hopeful face in the room and then he answered.

"Always."

Chapter 4: Token Errands

The plan easily came together, and it was a good plan. There was no sitting the bench on this one. For it to work, everyone had a part to play, and that participation would lead them across the barrier.

"We'll need Atlantis tokens for Jumper, Colby, Katie and Ann." Arden counted, "Four."

"Three. I've got the one that Keira gave me," Colby added.

Keira couldn't help but smile a little. She was glad it was back in his hands. It hung from a new brown leather cord around his neck. He rubbed it mindlessly.

"Do we really need more?" he asked. "I can use it; Keira can bring it back and hand it off to the next person."

"And what happens when we run into trouble and

one of you gets trapped on the other side without one. I'd rather not take the chance. It's best if everyone has a way to get back on their own."

Keira piped up, "I can get Mom's. She never uses it, so she won't notice that it's missing. That leaves us at two. Where can we find more?"

Ann looked at them hesitantly, "If we include William, he can pull across anyone that he's touching. We won't need coins."

"No!" Arden and Colby replied in unison.

Arden put a hand on Ann's back. "We cannot trust any mogdoc with this, especially a Gammen. Do you understand?"

"But he's helped us before," she protested.

Keira sighed and sat on the end of Ann's bed. "Ann, he's been manipulating us all along. Trust me; I've been the biggest fool of all. William was just the boy he was pretending to be. He is Brun, Brun Gammen. He took Drew. I know it."

"You don't believe that, do you?"

"It had to be him or Broo. She was distracting us, which only leaves..." Keira let the rest slide away. "I just don't know how, but I *know* it was him."

Colby stared at the floor. He knew it was Brun too.

"Then how are we supposed to round up two more? They're so rare," Ann worried.

"There's another. I can lay my hands on it, but it will be a bit dangerous and I will have to go alone. However, I believe it's worth the risk," Arden replied. "Ann will be discharged tonight. We can retrieve the coins and rendezvous at midnight to set our plan in motion."

"Good," Keira said. "But that's only three. Any

other ideas?"

"What about the other protector?" Katie asked, not even bothering to lift her head which found its way back into the magazine. "You know, that weird goth girl that had drivers' ed with Jump and Keira."

"Mikey," Jumper said a little too quickly.

Most of the kids at school called her Mikey, but her real name was Mikayla, Mikayla Collins. Mikey intimidated most people with her bold style and attitude, but Keira always felt like she was just misunderstood. She may have even admired Mikey a little.

"She's not weird," Keira said. "...Just a little different. Jump's different too, and you don't call him weird." A mischievous grin gradually made its way across her face. "Oh, maybe that's a bad example."

"Yeah, it is," Katie smirked. "I call Jumper weird. I'm just too mature to do it in front of you dweebs."

"Good one," Colby chuckled, and Jumper punched his shoulder.

Arden rolled his eyes. "Keira, speak to Mikayla Collins. You'll need a story or else she'll want to be involved. You must not allow it. This mission will take a delicate hand."

"She can be discreet," Keira said, her voice sounding slightly offended.

"A werewolf…discreet?" Arden laughed. It was big and bold and filled the room. A laugh from Arden was a rare occasion. Alone it would have caused their jaws to drop. However, this laugh was eclipsed by his preceding words which sparked an electric kind of excitement.

"No! Way!" Jumper yelled. "A real live werewolf?"

Ann mouthed to Keira, "Did you know?"

Keira shook her head.

Arden didn't notice Ann's question, he was still laughing too hard. He did catch the wrinkle that appeared across Keira's forehead.

"Oh, come now. You knew she was a wolf. She doesn't hide it. How could you not know? She has all the classic werewolf traits; buckets of attitude, advanced combat skills, and a love of danger."

"You've just described the football team."

Arden wiped the tears of laughter from his eyes. "I see, Keira, I suppose you are trying to say that it was not a natural conclusion for you. Still…"

His chest raised and fell again. "Discreet werewolf," he chuckled. "Next you'll tell me that vampires make great lifeguards."

"Vampires are real too!" Jumper shouted excitedly.

Keira glared at him. "Shouldn't we get moving on the plan instead of laughing at me?"

Arden closed his mouth and leaned to the doorway for support, suppressing the last threads of laughter to quiet giggles. He nodded simply, still trying to contain himself.

"Good," Keira said. "I'll grab Mom's token and talk to Mikey. Arden, you go and retrieve the one you know about. Ann and Katie, do whatever you need to do to prepare to open a portal for us. We all meet at the park at midnight."

"It's almost noon now. That's not even a full day to prepare," Arden warned.

"It will have to be enough."

"I think I should go with you when you talk to Mikey," Colby said. "Sounds like you might need a calming influence."

"Ooh, Ooh! I wanna go too," Jumper chimed in. "I've never met a werewolf before. Well, I've met Mikey before, but I didn't *know* she was a werewolf."

"Fine," Keira sighed. "Come on."

Jumper leaned over to kiss Ann on the forehead. He high-fived Colby as they left the room.

"Discreet werewolf," Arden laughed again.

* * *

"She could be anywhere. Where do we look first?" Colby asked as he rushed to keep up with the other two.

He quickly realized that his broken leg would be a hindrance, but was determined to not let it show. With each pained step he bit his lip harder.

Keira stopped short and the guys almost ran into her. The smile spread the width of her face as she turned to Colby.

“You have an idea,” Colby said as if it were a matter of fact.

It was. He could see it in that wide smile.

"I do," she smiled back. “If you were a party girl with a love of the moon and talent for trouble, where would you be at noon?"

Fifteen minutes later, they found themselves parked in front of a dilapidated house trailer just off the state highway. Keira ignored the “beware of dog” sign. She trailed through the tall grass, stepping over used car parts and random abandoned junk.

“Here goes,” she said and rapped on the thin door.

"Uhg, quit knocking. Whattaya want?" a female

voice grumbled from behind the door. Eyes peered through broken blinds.

"Is Mikey home?" Keira asked. Jumper and Colby stood behind her quietly.

"Who wants to know?"

"I go to school with her. My name's Keira, um Keira Ryan."

"You pullin' my leg?" the woman rasped.

However, she didn't have to answer. The woman with the gravelly voice was determined to see for herself. Keira overheard a series of clicks as the woman's fingers worked quickly to undo the locks.

"Mikayla! Get out here," she yelled before flinging the door open.

The too-skinny woman who welcomed them in looked as if she just rolled out of bed. She pushed tangled strands from her eyes and straightened her stained nightshirt, which barely covered the necessities.

"Sorry 'bout all that. Had I known you, of all people, *you* were coming," she kicked an empty pizza box away.

"Oh," Keira said, carefully stepping inside the door. The smell of cigarettes and stale chips nearly knocked her down. "It's fine, really, I won't be long."

"I just...I...I...can't believe you're here. I want you to know that the child of sun and moon is always, always, welcome in our humble home," she said sweetly. Then she turned her head and screamed, "Mikayla! Get up now!"

As Jumper and Colby filed in behind Keira, Mikey finally emerged from a back room, her eyes barely open. She stumbled into the kitchen area and grabbed a box of cereal, something with a cartoon character and every color in the rainbow. Colby raised an eyebrow at her boy boxers and tank top. She shuffled over to the couch and plopped down.

Keira could hear a "ha" under Jumper's breath.

"Mikayla Eileen Collins!" the woman stomped her foot. "The child of sun and moon is here, and she needs you."

"No, there's no emergency," Keira added, shooting a sideways glance at Colby and Jumper.

The woman ignored her and continued screaming at Mikey. "You get your lazy butt off that couch. Her life depends on it."

"Really, it's nothing," Keira shook her head.

"Geez, drama queen, look at her. She's fine," Mikey said before popping a cereal square into the air and catching it in her mouth.

"I'm so sorry for my daughter's rudeness. I don't know what ta do with her. Won't ya'll come on in and sit down?"

"Oh no, I...." Keira started, but her sentence lingered.

"We just came to pick up Mikey to work on a group project for school," Colby assisted.

Keira nodded.

"Yeah, the *group* project," Mikey rolled her eyes. "I'll be gone awhile. Don't wait up."

Mikey balanced the cereal box on top of the clutter on the coffee table, which wasn't a coffee table at all as Keira had first thought, but several neatly-stacked empty beer cartons. Mikey headed toward the door.

"Don't you need to change first?" Colby asked.

In a move so quick that it could only be supernatural, Mikey snatched his collar and pulled him close.

"Wanna come help me, teacher's pet?"

* * *

"...Let me come in," Arden finished the entry phrase.

The sand below him opened up and he dropped into his old mentor's home.

Truth be told, it was not only her home, but her office, and her entire life for that matter. Nedda was the keeper of the official guardian archives. This place housed all that information.

It was also stored within Nedda herself. She locked away every fact and every figure in her mind and it forced her into insanity. She was literally driven mad by the details.

Arden's apprenticeship ended early when Nedda became too dangerous. Her madness clouded her judgment. She now saw him as an enemy, convinced that he was the one that had done this to her.

Arden's last visit to Nedda hadn't been that long ago, less than a year. On that visit, she nearly killed him. She was probably worse now. Perhaps she would get a second try.

He knew the risks, but couldn't stay away. Coming for the Atlantis token was just an excuse. They could get everyone across the barrier, one at a time, with one coin just as Colby suggested. It would take a while, but it could be done.

No, the reason he found himself in this place wasn't the coin. He had to see her again. This time he would be smarter.

On his last visit he noticed that despite her

insanity, she was keeping to routine. He had lived there long enough to know it. He knew when she worked, when she ate, when she slept. He slipped in an hour after her usual bedtime.

Arden tucked his head and rolled to his feet as soon as he landed. The room was dark. There was no sign of her.

He pulled two small knives, one in each palm. His large hands concealed them easily. If he came upon her, she wouldn't feel threatened, and he would have the means to protect himself should he need it.

Each footstep seemed unnecessarily loud. He reached down and used one of the knives to pry his shoes off, careful not to let them fall to the floor. He arranged them side by side, leaving them out of the way, against the wall. Arden continued down the hall in his socked feet.

Darkness stretched past the corridor and spilled into the adjoining rooms. Every light turned out; every door shut tight. Even the magic that laced the windows was dimmed to match twilight.

Nearing the last of the windows, Arden admonished himself for a fleeting thought about the filth collected on his fresh, white socks. After all, he had more important things to worry about.

Another step took him into the study. Books towered over him on all sides. He couldn't see them, but he knew they were there. They were always there. The thought of them gave him comfort.

Unlike the others, this room was windowless. Not a spec of light dwelled within it. The designers had purposely planned it that way so that the archived pages would not be exposed to light, natural or magical.

He placed a hand out and ran it over the familiar volumes. He closed his eyes and pictured the books in his head as he ran his fingers over the leather covers and embossed titles. He had shelved those books dozens, if not hundreds, of times. It didn't matter how long he had been away. He knew this study like his own body.

Arden breathed, taking in the scent of the pages. It took every ounce of restraint in him not to settle into a seat in the corner with one of his favorites. It was something he used to do often. Used to do...in the past, he reminded himself.

That was not who he was now. Now, he was the mentor of the child of sun and moon. Now, he was on a mission to help her bring forth the fall of the House of Gammen.

Arden took three steps more, then two side-steps to avoid the table he knew was positioned in the center of the room. He reached out to prove himself right. When his hand touched polished oak, he smiled to himself. He quietly jogged a couple more steps into the next room.

He hadn't realized that he was holding his breath.

At attention in the doorway, the silence gripped him. It wasn't a good thing. Nedda, the once sweet curator of the official guardian archives, was a chronic snorer.

* * *

"Mikayla!" the woman screeched.

Mikey had hold of Colby's collar. He didn't back away as he scrambled to recall every tidbit he had ever read about wolves.

Surely the rules for wolf encounters must also apply to werewolves, he thought.

"Mikayla!"

Mikey's long sigh settled into a pout. "Maybe next time." She straightened his collar and dusted his shoulders before strutting to the back room to change.

Jumper stifled a chuckle forcing Colby to jab him in the ribs not-so discreetly.

"Sorry again 'bout her," the woman said. "I hate that she bothered yer special boys."

"Special boys?" Colby asked.

"Well, my nose is much older than Mikayla's, but even I can tell why the guardian keeps you two close. I just never heard of one havin' two before."

"I'm sorry. What are we talking about? Two what?" Keira intervened.

"Charges, of course. Thought I picked up a hint of vox magic inside 'em. No? Maybe it's just vanilla. It smells 'bout the same."

"You're crazy, old woman," Mikey appeared from nowhere. Her midnight black hair pulled back so that they could now see the new electric blue strands underneath. In only minutes, she had dramatically transformed. The sleepwear was long gone, replaced by skintight black snakeskin pants and a slick blue corset with satin ribbons. The corset matched the highlights in her hair and didn't quite meet the top of her pants so that her golden navel ring peeked out between.

"I told you before," Mikey warned as she pulled on a pair of combat boots. "Keira's charge was kidnapped by the Unionists and it doesn't matter, he's just a midnight child. Quit sniffing my guests."

All color flushed from the woman's face. "Do not

call him that. You will not use that language in front of her, ya hear me?"

"Ugh, yeah, I hear you," Mikey rolled her eyes for the umpteenth time.

After a last, extra-strong yank of her boot laces, she tucked her arm under Keira's and pulled her out the door with Jumper and Colby in tow. Keira was mesmerized by the crystal skulls hanging from Mikey's ears. Before they got to Colby's car, Keira came to her senses and stopped.

"How did you know my charge was taken?"

"Helloooo. I'm one of your protectors. It's kinda my job to know."

"Well," Keira shuffled. "He's not a midnight child. He's the real deal."

"Whatever you say."

"...And I don't think it was the Unionists that took him."

"Good. We're on the same page."

"Then why did you..."

"I got my reasons," Mikey interrupted. "So lay the heavy on me. What are you doing here?"

"No, heavy," Colby rushed. "Everything's fine."

"Right," Mikey sized them up. "The jock's heart is pounding so fast, I can barely hear myself think."

The corner of Jumper's mouth pulled up into a mischievous smile. “Dude, she can hear my heart. That’s awesome.”

Mikey didn't look at the boys. Instead she focused on Keira, looking for signs of stress, inviting the clues to show themselves.

"Like you said, 'everything's fine.' Her charge was taken, the Empress is losing control, and the Elders have essentially tied our prophecy girl's hands.

I'm sure everything is just peachy."

"You're totally right," Keira said, and Mikey raised an eyebrow. "Things are *not* good. I need to take Colby across the barrier. He's practically a genius, and if anyone can figure out the prophecy, it's him."

"Yeah, so, what are you doing here?" Mikey pushed.

"I need to borrow a coin."

Mikey backed up a step and put her hands on her hips. Colby held his breath.

"An Atlantis token," Mikey corrected. "Real rare. What makes you think I have one?"

"Do you have one or not?" Jumper stepped in.

"Back down, jock boy. You don't want to start something you can't finish."

She never broke eye contact with Keira. "I got one," she said carefully. "But I'm not buying this whole research act. You could bring the book here. He doesn't have to go there. My guess is that you're plotting something big. I want in."

* * *

Arden moved silently into Nedda's bedroom. Unlike the study, this room hosted two enchanted windows like those found in other parts of her home. Like those other rooms, these windows were dimmed to mimic late twilight.

Even the small amount of light that the windows provided would be a huge advantage. This was her private, inner sanctum. He didn't know her bedroom like he knew the other rooms. However, he did know one thing about it. He knew that beside her bed was a table. On that table was a box. In that box was an Atlantis token.

Arden flattened his body to the wall just inside the bedroom door and stayed there for a moment to survey his surroundings. This part of the house, like the portion he had already navigated, was as neat as a pin. Insanity obviously didn't affect her housekeeping abilities.

Perhaps it was part of the madness, he thought. He assumed that someone could have a compulsive disorder that led them to such action. Before he came to live with the Ryans, he didn't know that such a thing existed. Then, Keira introduced him to something that she called "reality" shows.

He dropped to his knees knowing that he would be harder to detect if he were crawling. The room was carpeted, allowing him silent movement across the floor. The silence chilled him. Somewhere inside he knew that it was too quiet.

Crawling proved difficult with a knife in each hand. He tucked one between his teeth and stuck the other in the back of his belt. Only he missed the belt and the knife dropped to the floor. Hitting the carpet, it made a soft, dense thud. Arden froze.

"You better pick that up," came a whisper from the dark. "Five, six, pick up sticks."

Arden collapsed to his stomach and picked up the knife as he rolled and rolled. He rolled right under the bed before he stopped.

Nedda's laughter rose around him. It did not warm him or make him feel safe as it did when he was younger. This laugh was off, creepy somehow, and it seemed to come from nowhere and everywhere at once. Under the bed, he laid on his stomach with a knife in each hand. No training had ever prepared him for this.

A couple of loud bangs drew his attention. His eyes scanned the floor. Nothing. A hiss sounded and fire bloomed in the fireplace to his left. Surprised, he jolted up and cracked his head on one of the boards supporting the mattress springs. Pushing past the pain, and mouthing a few expletives in the process, Arden tightened his grip on the knives. The fire's flickering light danced on the walls, but did not reach the door.

Arden quickly assessed his options. One, wait her out then get what he came for. Two, hope she isn't blocking the door and make a run for it. Three, move now, demand the token, and take whatever comes. Brave or foolish or both? As he stumbled over the thought, something grabbed his foot and yanked.

"Catch a tiger by the toe!" Nedda yelled.

She dragged him from beneath the bed and toward the fireplace. Arden stabbed the floor and held on tight. The sudden stop threw her off balance and she fell to the floor; pink fuzzy slippers in the air.

Arden raced to the end table by the bed. He scooped up the intricately-carved wooden box and tucked it like a football in one arm. From the corner of his eye, he could see Nedda rolling to her feet as he jumped over the bed. When he landed on the other side, he turned to look. She wasn't there.

A slam turned his attention forward. It was the bedroom door. All the lights went out. Arden froze.

He took a step toward the door. Nothing happened. Another step.

"Tut, tut, tut. That's not where the box goes." Nedda's voice was close...too close...right at his ear. He felt her warm breath on his neck.

"Oh, this box?" he said, trying his best to act non-threatening, despite the knives in his belt. "I'm just going to take a quick peek inside."

"Oh for heaven's sake," she said. She snatched the box from him and disappeared into the darkness. He breathed heavy, unsure of what to do. Then, the lamp came on.

Nedda was sitting under the light in a rocking chair with the box squarely in her lap. "I raised you better than this, boy. Where are your manners? All you had to do was ask. But you, *you* break into my home and roll around on the floor like a commando."

His head quirked to the side like a dog when it hears an odd sound. "I...um."

"You've come for a token," she says more to herself than to him. She nods to the air above her head. "Yes, obviously. She'll need to stop the Harvest."

* * *

"That's the offer. Take it or leave it." Mikey looked as if she was already getting bored with the conversation.

It was a package deal, the token *and* Mikey. Keira knew what Arden had said. She knew that Mikey wasn't to be involved. Then, her eyes lifted and met Jumper and Colby's. If she left now, without a token, one of them wouldn't have a direct lifeline home. If she took Mikey's offer, she'd still need another token. She'd still have fewer tokens than humans. Wait, no--Mikey wasn't human.

"Listen, there's no point in borrowing the token, if you'll have to use it. So just forget it," Keira tested her.

"Hold on," Mikey started to back down. "Don't get hasty. I can't even use the token. Duh. Your ancestors saw to that. Only guardians and token-carrying humans can cross the barrier."

"Then why do you have it in the first place?" Jumper asked.

"Insurance," her mouth barely moved as the word slipped out of a smirk. "Besides, I'm tired of sitting the bench. Come on, we better get going. I don't know what kind of time schedule you're on, but it will take us a while to retrieve the token."

"I didn't say you could come with us," Keira jogged to catch up. Mikey was already opening the passenger door to Colby's car.

"No, you didn't," she agreed and sat down and slammed the door closed.

Colby shot Keira a quick look before climbing into the driver's seat. Keira grabbed the handle of the back door directly behind Mikey.

Jumper yelled over to her from the other side of the car. "Guess you've met your match," he laughed. "She's even more bull-headed than you are."

He disappeared inside the car.

"We'll just see about that," Keira said to herself before climbing in to join them.

* * *

"The Harvest?" Arden repeated.

"Ah, did you forget? Distracted by the big picture? The big picture is constant. It's the details that get us every time. And what a good student, I thought you were. Pity."

"Nedda, please focus. Stay with me. Will the Empress re-invoke the Harvest?"

"She must. Not a real Empress without one. But then again, she's not really a mogdoc anyway, not wholly. Wholly, wholly, wholly. Quite a funny word. A workout for the entire mouth. I love the way it makes my tongue feel. Wholly, wholly, wholly," she giggled as she over exaggerated the pronunciation of the word.

After the twentieth "wholly" Arden grew impatient. "Please, may I borrow your Atlantis token for the child of sun and moon?"

"Alright. Here it is, grumbly pants."

She reached into the box and tossed the token to him. He caught it by the long, thin chain on which it was attached. He stared at it and smiled, realizing that no matter how insane she had become, she was still helping him, looking out for him.

"Thank you, Nedda."

"Borrow and steal are cats and dogs."

"Uhh, right," he replied hesitantly, thinking it was best to just go with it. "I promise I will bring this back in proper condition."

Her eyes fell sadly. "Better not come back. I don't think her mind is right," Nedda said. “Besides you’ve already lost.”

* * *

To say the next hour in the car was awkward would be an understatement. Mental torture. That's what it felt like. Unrelenting boredom set to a soundtrack of pounding death metal rock.

Keira stared out the window. Her mind occupied

itself, thinking over what was to come. Jumper closed his eyes, apparently exhausted by the adrenaline rush of meeting a real werewolf. Mikey rolled down the window and waved her hand over the rushing air in sync with the music. Every once in a while she would mouth a few words or drum with her fingers.

Colby checked the rear view mirror repeatedly. It wasn't the traffic that had him worried. He had the mirror set so that he could see Keira. She was growing more impatient by the minute. Keira had a terrible habit of holding her emotions until they exploded. Colby could practically see the countdown scroll across her forehead.

Mikey was leading the way. They drove straight out of town on the interstate. It was the only four-lane road in the county. Unlike the others, the interstate lacked the familiar dips and turns of the Ohio River valley. Its path was straight and the scenery unchanging.

After nearly an hour, Mikey said, "This one." Colby exited the highway and followed the ramp to a winding country road. The road was quickly enveloped by the woods, changing over from modern blacktop to dirt and gravel. A cloud of dust rose up as they continued on, twisting and turning around hillsides and over streams. Colby winced at the thought of the dust settling on his clean car.

Keira thought they had reached their destination when they approached a two-story shack with chickens milling about. It was the only civilization she had seen for miles. That was a false assumption. Colby followed a hairpin turn to the right and they continued deeper into the forest.

After another two miles, the road was swallowed

completely by the trees.

"Here's the part where we go on foot, kiddos," Mikey smiled. She hopped out of the car.

The others didn't move. The engine continued to purr.

"You know, we could just leave her here," Keira suggested, but they were all thinking it.

Mikey rapped on the hood.

"Let's go before the werewolf destroys my paint job," Colby sighed.

"Man, I'd pay to see *that* on your insurance claim form," Jumper added.

They piled out of the car and followed Mikey into the woods. The air was heavy with moisture and a mixed scent of pine, decaying leaves, and honeysuckle.

The gang was surprised to find that Mikey was actually following an established path; a rudimentary one, but a path all the same, free of poison ivy and lined with decaying landscaping timbers. The beginning boasted a near forty-five degree incline. Mikey, Keira, and even Jumper took it in stride, but Colby fell back. The hill proved too treacherous to maneuver with one good leg. Keira doubled back to him.

"It's too steep. I can't," Colby heaved.

"I'll stay with you."

"Keira, I'll be fine. You're the one who'll be with a werewolf."

"Go back to the car. We'll meet you there in a few minutes," Keira said.

"Hurry it up, lovebirds. We're losin' daylight," Mikey yelled back to them.

"We're not lovebirds," the two yelled in unison.

"Go," Colby said.

She took off to catch up with Mikey and Jumper. They were just cresting the hill, about to disappear to the other side. By the time Keira reached them, they had stopped.

"Come on, let's keep moving," Keira said. They were unmoved. Keira looked ahead to see what captivated them. It was a natural waterfall. Sparkling water rushed over rocks jabbed into the hillside. The waters collected into a pool at the bottom. More of the same rocks, only with moss, surrounded the waterfall. Keira closed her eyes. It sounded like the shower in the morning, when she would wait for warm water to reach the pipes. Without warning, Jumper took off down the hillside. His shirt and excited shouts flew into the air. At the water's edge, he kicked off his flip flops and dove in.

"Dumb jock," Mikey laughed.

* * *

Arden's breath caught. "What? What did you say?"

"You've already lost," Nedda repeated. "No, no, how silly of me. You have stolen…stolen the lost," she laughed. "And yet it's not found!"

She made a clicking noise with her tongue and closed the box. He put the chain around his neck for safekeeping and started to leave. He stopped when he reached the doorway. She was following close behind, probably making sure that he was actually leaving.

"Nedda," he turned to her and reached out to touch her wrinkled hands. She ushered him into the hallway. Her eyes, bright as those of a curious child, looked into his as he continued, "If there's ever anything that you need, or if you would just want someone to talk to..."

"The Harvest, the five, and the fall," she whispered.

"What?"

"TooooDALLOOO!"

She smacked a button hidden within the wallpaper pattern. Glass partitions sprang from the wall and sectioned Arden off from her. He pounded on the glass, but she just waved. With a whoosh of air, he was ejected from Nedda's home, landing on the beach shoeless and with the token around his neck.

* * *

"Good thing you brought him along though," Mikey said, the left corner of her mouth turned up in a satisfied smirk. "At least we won't have to get wet."

When the redhead came up for air, he found Keira and Mikey sitting on the rocks. Mikey reached in her corset and pulled out a plastic baggie.

"What's that?" Keira asked.

"Bunyip treats," she answered like it was the most normal thing in the world. "They're actually quite tasty."

Keira took a step back.

"What's a bunyip?" Jump asked, his arms circling him as he tread water.

"Like a dog," Mikey said.

Keira gave her a sideways glance. "Jump, maybe you should get out of the water."

"No, no," Mikey interrupted. "He's perfectly safe and one of us is going to have to get in. Jock boy's already wet."

"*Like* a dog?"

"Well, yeah, his face looks like a dog, but he's got flippers and tusks. You know, a bunyip," she shrugged. She tossed a wafer onto the rocks a few feet away and whistled. "No sudden movements, jock."

"Where is it?"

"Not it, *he*. I call him Lucky," Mikey said proudly.

"And where is Lucky now?"

"Oh, he's been watching you from the moment you jumped in." She looked past him. "Who's a good boy?"

"Jump," Keira said, not that he was a good boy. She said it as she pointed to a dark inset behind the waterfall. Jumper looked that way and caught a sudden chill from the yellow eyes that stared back.

"Here boy, it's me. I've got some treats for you." Mikey held another wafer in the air.

A snout covered in dark fur moved from the shadows and let out a low bellow. Keira pulled the dagger from her ankle.

"A woman of action," Mikey smiled. "Like it, but put that thing away."

Keira regarded her, "I'll keep it in my hand just in case. Thanks anyway."

"Whatever," Mikey said.

"Hey, guys?"

Lucky splashed into the water. His head remained just above the surface, razor sharp tusks extended.

"Guys?" Jumper prompted again.

Mikey moved to the side of the pool, tempting her guard dog with the wafer in her hand. Lucky changed his course, bearing toward her.

"Jock, look for a metal case, behind the waterfall. Go. Now," Mikey said softly, though her eyes showed the urgency. She tossed Lucky a wafer and he caught it in mid-air. "Hurry."

"A silver case?"

"Silver? You've got to be kidding me. I'm a freaking werewolf. Get a brain."

Jumper shot her his "duh" look. "Then what?"

"Iron, jock boy. Iron keeps the fairies out. Does it matter? It's a waterfall, not a department store. Not like there's going to be more than one to choose from. Just go!"

Jumper dove under the water, and as he did, Lucky turned his direction.

"Here, boy," Mikey called again, bringing his attention back to her with another wafer.

Keira spotted Jumper as he pulled himself up into the dark inset where Lucky had been perched. A moment later, he waved a small, heavy box in the air.

"We don't need the box, just the coin," Keira reminded him.

He opened the box and pulled the tiny copper item from it. No chain or cord. Jumper bit onto it and closed his mouth around it. He dove back into the water.

This time, Mikey couldn't hold Lucky's attention.

Lucky shot through the water like a torpedo. Keira kicked off her boots and dove in after them, her dagger still in her hand.

"It's fine. He's harmless," Mikey was shouting from the bank.

Keira came up for air right in front of Jumper.

"Where did he go?" she asked.

Jumper was shaking his pale, terrified face.

"Slowly then," Keira whispered, pushing her long hair behind her ears with her free hand.

He put a hand on her shoulder and she nearly jumped out of her skin.

"Take this," he said through the side of his mouth. He reached in and pulled the token out and handed it to her. "Just in case."

"Keep it," she said. "We're both getting out of here. Follow me."

They floated slowly across the pool. Keira tried to keep an ear out for the bunyip, but the rushing waters of the waterfall didn't allow for it. There was no sign of Lucky as they came to the edge.

"See," Mikey said, hands on her hips. "He just likes to play."

Keira tossed her dagger up on the mossy rock. She reached back for Jumper and pulled him toward the edge.

"That was close. Thanks. I…"

He was gone, pulled under the water's surface before he could finish the thought.

Keira gulped in a breath before she disappeared after him. Under the water, the sound of the falls lowered an octave. Its sound pounded in her ears. Then, something deeper rang and held like the final note of a song sung long ago.

She twisted frantically, searching for Jumper. Bubbles rose up at her sides. Rocks. Plants. No Jumper.

Keira breeched the surface, sucking new air into her lungs.

"Over there," Mikey yelled out.

Amidst frantic splashes, Jumper took his own

panicked breaths. Keira kicked out, reaching the spot, just as Lucky took him back under.

Another breath and she followed. The beast rolled with Jumper as he kicked helplessly. Keira punched at its head and it roared, the force of it came at her body like a current pushing her deeper into the water.

She fought it back to the surface and caught another quick breath. Her dagger. She reached down to her ankle, but it wasn't there. Too late she remembered tossing it onto the rocks.

She pulled her body up to dive back under, but everything became eerily still. Lucky had stopped rolling. Everything stopped. This only propelled her back under with more urgency than before.

As she broke the water's surface, the solid note she heard earlier as if it were part of some forgotten song, rang louder than before.

Lucky uncurled himself from Jumper's limp body and paddled away, back to his cave in the rocks behind the waterfall.

Keira reached out. Jumper's eyes popped open.

They broke through the surface, spattering up water from their lungs. Keira dragged Jumper to the bank and with a tremendous shove he was out of the water and lying in the sun.

Keira crawled onto the rock and rested on her knees as she choked out the water still caught in her throat.

"You're welcome," she heard Mikey say.

A smile played across the werewolf's lips as she held up a small instrument which resembled a miniature flute. At first glance, Keira thought it was metal as it shined in the sun, but she soon realized it wasn't. It was seashell.

"Siren whistle, see. I told you he was harmless. He just wants to play."

Jumper's coughs turned into a laugh. He rolled onto his back and held up the smashed copper coin.

Chapter 5:
In, Under & Around the Citadel

The scent of orange and ginger meat roasting over an open flame was nearly choked out by the stench of the alley. Even in the ever present darkness, buyers and sellers packed the market. Low voices rumbled in heated negotiation over things like food and weapons, lit only by a sprinkling of strategically placed torches on the towering outer block walls of the Citadel. Its stone surface rough and dark, much like its inhabitants.

The night was warm, season-less, like it always is on the other side of the barrier. Once they retrieved all the tokens, crossing the barrier was easy. Ann and Keira now kept watch over the scene from a secure rooftop above the marketplace just outside the Mogdoc Citadel, the home of Empress Broo Gammen.

A light breeze drifted past and lifted Keira's hair. She moved the stray strands from her face and as she did, her eyes wandered to the pitch black sky.

"Do you think they miss them?" Keira asked with a sigh.

"Who misses what?" Ann replied, unable and unwilling to tear her eyes away from her watch duty.

"The stars," Keira said. "Do you think the mogdocs miss them? It depresses me every time I'm here and I don't even live here."

Ann shrugged, "I don't suppose they have a choice. It's not like they can leave Atlantis. Anyway, I doubt they really care."

Keira nodded. She could understand. The mogdocs didn't seem to care about anything but themselves.

Ann focused through her binoculars on a man just outside the torchlight, near the gates that led to the non-public interior of the Empress's Citadel. The man would have been hard to see if he wasn't wearing white. She held her breath and focused on him as he started to move. Reaching from beneath a white unionist robe, Jumper Johnson lifted an arm. Bianca's stolen Atlantis token dangled from his wrist as he flashed two fingers in the air twice.

"Two guards on each side," Ann relayed to Keira.

Keira nodded, finally bringing herself back to the job at hand. She focused back on Jumper Johnson's white robe in the marketplace below them.

Ann elbowed her, "You with me?"

"Just thinking about all it took to get here. I sure hope this works."

"Don't worry," Ann said with a pat on her friends back. "We have a plan, remember?"

After Keira nodded, the Traveler's eyes moved to an old man, hobbling on his cane. His clothes were clean but oversized and ragged. They dragged on the ground due to the fact that his back was hunched over. Ann and Keira watched as the man slowly made his way up the alley, jingling with every step. He stopped a couple of times to peruse merchandise along the way, but never bought a thing. As he approached the gates, Arden swept past the old man, relieving him of the full bag of coins tied at his waist.

The old man reached out, but Arden was too fast. Two of the Citadel guards, eyeing the take for themselves, pushed the old man to the ground and took chase after Arden.

The old man screeched at the remaining two guards. Jumper maneuvered over to them to help the man up and join in the argument.

"Now," Ann said. She took Keira's hand and in the next second, they were at the gates, slipping inside the Citadel past the distracted guards.

Inside the gates of the Citadel, Keira and Ann quickly padded across the courtyard to the main building. A moment later, Katie appeared with Arden inside the gates. They too rushed to the cover of the main building, finding the girls along the wall.

Arden moved in front of them to lead the way. "If I'm right," he whispered. "We should be able to tap into the tunnel that Ann and I used the last time we were here."

Ann shuddered. She couldn't help it. The memory of her time in the Citadel gave her a chill. The last time she set foot in the mogdoc capital was because Brun brought her there to rescue Arden. Brun turned on her and delivered her to the mogdocs, but it was just a way to sneak her into position to rescue Arden. Or was it? Did he really betray her or was it just all part of the plan? She didn't know for sure.

What she did know was that after the mogdocs captured her, she was able to get to Arden and several human prisoners held in the depths of the Citadel. They freed the prisoners and got them out using an escape tunnel that Ann had discovered. After their great escape, the mogdocs sealed the exit of the escape tunnel, so that no one could return.

However, Arden had done his research. In speaking with those that escaped, he found that the tunnel took them across the bottom of the well.

"I'm hoping the mogdocs don't recognize the well as a point of entry or maybe they forgot about it," he said.

"Or are too conceited to think we can get inside the gates to use it," Ann added.

"Let us hope that is the case." Arden pulled a rope from his pack. "Who wants the first go at it?"

"Do you have to ask?" Keira grinned.

The old-fashioned water well had a wench that lowered a wooden bucket on a heavy, thick rope that looked very much like the ones that they use on ships in old pirate movies. Thick as it was, it looked like it was original to the well. Ann was relieved that Arden had enough foresight to bring his own nylon rock climbing rope.

Arden looped one end around the wench support while Keira fastened the carabiner on the other end around her. When she was ready, Arden lowered her into the well.

A curving block wall surrounded her as she descended from night into total darkness. She fought the urge to hum or whistle, anything to disrupt the deadly quiet of the space. Once she was low enough that the light of her flashlight wouldn't be seen from the surface, she flicked it on. She shone it below. The water, like glass, rested a good twenty to thirty feet beneath her dangling toes.

Arden had slowed and was now stopping briefly after every half foot or so. He must have thought that the pass-through was close. Keira ran the light over the walls. It was all the same smooth block.

When her feet splashed in the water, she yanked on the rope. Arden stopped. It was all block, the same block, smooth and hard and going on forever. Keira gave the rope two tugs, their agreed upon signal for "up".

Keira's mind raced with possible next steps. If this entrance was sealed, the mogdocs had probably taken other precautions too. They would have to step very carefully.

She continued to spray the flashlight's beam over the walls as she ascended on the unlikely chance that she had missed the tunnel. As she approached the opening, she shut the light off. The last thing they needed was to draw the attention of the mogdoc guard.

The instant her light disappeared, the rope stopped moving. Keira held still for a moment before giving the rope another two tugs. She looked up, but there was nothing to see. Water still dripping from her shoes bared the only sound.

She gripped the rope, readying herself to climb out. Then, without warning, the supporting end came rushing toward her. Keira plunged down, down, down, into the abyss. There was no time to scream; only time to take a sustaining breath and hold it tight.

The mogdoc guards rushed them at the top of the well. Arden braced a foot against the rock base and held onto the rope with one hand. With the other hand, he stretched out for his pack. Ann jumped before him, foil at the ready, but it was too late. One of the mogdocs let loose an arrow. It was a perfect hit, splitting the rope in one shot. Arden lunged after it, reaching it seconds too late.

Ann yelled, "Get out of here!" to Katie before tackling a mogdoc that appeared in front of them. Katie sprinted toward the outer wall.

Choosing a spot without the benefit of torchlight, she slammed up against the cold stone and rolled so that her back was to it. Under the darkness, she could see the action at the well. The heaving of her lungs competed with her racing heart. Still she found the breath to scream when her view was eclipsed.

"What are you doing here?" Brun Gammen demanded.

He was hidden too well by the darkness. He kept his voice low. She quickly realized that, like her, he didn't want to be seen either. She remembered how her parents had warned her about the "Lost Prince". She knew Keira had her doubts about him. However, in this instant, his eyes, though a mogdoc green, sparkled with what looked like concern.

"We're here for Drew," she whispered back. "Help us."

"No," he shook his head and stared at her like he could will her request to change. "No. No. No."

Katie didn't know how she should respond, so she just shrugged her shoulders apologetically. He placed his hands on them.

"You have to leave," he said. "Now. You'll ruin

everything."

"We're not leaving without Drew…or Keira."

"Keira's here too? Of course, she is," he breathed, the sound of it thick with aggravation. The concerned kindness Katie had seen in his eyes earlier quickly vanished.

"Take this."

With inhuman speed, he swung the long, black coat he was wearing from his form and wrapped her in it. He pulled a small device from the collar and spoke into it.

"All perimeter guards, report to the Throne Room immediately. The Citadel has been breached. I repeat, the Citadel has been breached."

"What are you doing?" Katie smacked the device from his hand. It made a slight thunk as it dented the hard dirt ground.

With a hand on her chest, he thrust her into the wall with a little more force than necessary. An involuntary whimper escaped her lips.

"I was securing your escape. Now all the guards will swarm the Throne Room to protect Broo, leaving you a clear exit," he said. "Next time think before you lash out, brat."

He cringed as the all too familiar words came on their own, a phrase that his father must have spouted a million times and everyone one of those times it was emphasized with a show of brute force. He pulled his hand back quickly.

"Watch it, jerk!" Katie shrieked.

He unclenched his jaw and looked to the ground. "I'm sorry, now go. And next time your sister tells you to run, don't panic and run, use your gift as she intended."

Katie shrugged off his unwanted advice, but he still continued, "If you're going to do it the human way, follow the wall. There's an exit just past the corner. I called the guards in, so you shouldn't run into any trouble."

"What about the others?" she pointed to Arden and Ann, still fighting the small mogdoc contingent that had discovered them at the well.

"I'll do what I can. That's all I can promise."

"Brun, William, whoever you are, are you really on our side?"

He realized that not one of them had ever come out and asked him that, not even Keira. Katie's candor was not something he was used to hearing on the mogdoc side of the barrier. He was used to words full of deceit and double meaning. She felt the full weight of Brun's eyes as he considered her words.

"I'm on my side. That's what we mogdocs do, right?" he finally spat out. "Now go, before you no longer have the option."

She stared at him.

"Go!" he yelled.

With an incredulous humph, she turned her back on him and hurried along the wall, clutching her locket nervously.

He watched the girl leave, his coat dragging the ground behind her. Knowing she was well on her way to safety, he turned his attention back to the duo at the well.

They didn't need his help after all. They had shaped up to be excellent fighters, he thought. From his darkened spot at the wall, he watched them incapacitate the guards. It wasn't until they started tying up their rivals that he realized Keira wasn't with them.

Brun couldn't approach them. He knew that he came to blows with the Brit every time they met. He had often thought about using his diplomatic ties to get Keira a new mentor. This one seemed too pig-headed and careless. If he had the job, he would never let her out of his sight. He could see that Ann, one of Keira's protectors, did no better. Did they both abandon the child of sun and moon?

Ann pulled tight the last knot and sprang to her feet. She rushed to the well and leaned over its edge. Brun watched with curiosity wondering what it was that she had found there. Only when he heard Ann's shouts, he understood that it was not some*thing* found, but some*one* lost. Keira.

The thought of Keira falling into that deep stone well moved his feet without intention. In a flash, he was at the well's edge beside Ann.

"Did she fall? Did one of them push her into the well?" he rushed.

"Ahhh!" Ann yelped, startled by his sudden appearance.

Arden was equally startled, but instead of screaming, he acted. He already had a poisoned dagger at the prince's back. Brun spun on him and knocked him to the ground.

"This isn't about you, tooth mouse," he said.

Arden growled like a hungry wolf, as he dusted himself off and came to his feet. "It never was," he warned.

"Not helping," Ann huffed. "She's in there. She might be hurt. I can't hear her."

Brun leaned over the edge again. There was no sign of her.

Arden brushed him aside. "Lower me down," he said, handing Ann the remaining nylon rope. "If he tries anything funny while I'm down there, you have my permission to knife him, royalty or not. We'll worry about the diplomacy of it later."

"No," Brun put a hand out to stop him. "You make a very good point, rat. I am royalty, and this is *my* well. If anyone goes down there it will be me. There's a tunnel that runs into the side of the well, I will access it from there. If she is hurt, it will be much safer to extract her using the tunnel."

Ann and Arden looked at each other. Their sudden silence forced reckoning on Brun.

"That's why she's down there, isn't it. The little one said that you were here for Drew. She was trying to find the tunnel to get inside."

His eyes locked on Arden, looking for the slightest twitch to confirm his theory. He almost didn't hear Ann's tiny request.

"Little one? What did you do to my sister?"

"I helped her get out. You two should follow. The alarm has been sounded. The whole Citadel knows that there are enemies on site. It is not safe for you here. Go. I'll get to Keira, you have my word."

"The word of a mogdoc," Arden snorted.

"Yes, rat, you have the word of a mogdoc," he glared back.

"And what about Drew? Do you guarantee his safety too? I suppose that as his kidnapper, you can do that."

"Do what you wish," Brun finally answered, tired of the game.

He sprinted away, presumable to enter the main building of the Citadel, leaving a very confused Ann and a very irritated Arden behind.

Far below them, Keira coughed as she came to the frigid water's surface. The frayed end of the rope that once held her body now swirled in the well water. The top of the well was but a mere pinpoint of dim light. Complete darkness surrounded her. She pointed her toes, seeking the bottom, but there was none to be found.

"Wait, my flashlight. It should float. It's got to be here somewhere. Why am I talking to myself?"

She pushed through the water, a new chilling sensation with each stroke. Keira heard a thunk against the wall. She reached toward it and wrapped her fingers around the familiar plastic. She put a foot out to push off the slimy well wall. Only her foot never hit the wall.

She kicked at it again. Still nothing stopped her foot as it traveled past where it should have hit block.

"The water level changed," Keira whispered, even though she didn't have to. The tunnel was right there. Flooded, but there.

She looked up. There was no way to scale the smooth walls. The only way to get out was the tunnel, but she had no way of knowing how much of the tunnel was underwater. Could she survive the swim? Even if she survived it, she would be in the heart of the Mogdoc Empire alone.

She closed her eyes and let her head fall back onto the water to think. After all, the tunnel wasn't going anywhere.

He's close, she thought. *I can feel it. Just in and out. That's all there is to it. Just in and out. They know we were here. They might move him. We might never get this close again.*

Inhaling deep, Keira flicked on the flashlight and dove under the water into the tunnel.

Chapter 6:
Look What the Shapeshifter Dragged In

Keira burst through the water's surface. She sucked in a lung-full of musty air, and immediately choked on it. The well was now long behind her. The flashlight's beam traced the walls. Nothing there but rock and algae.

Keira continued on, kicking her legs out and pushing through the water like the frogs she would watch at the river's edge when she was little. Colby would never pick them up, citing a million different reasons except for the real one. Keira would pick a frog up from time to time, but she too would usually leave them alone. She would sit for hours; just watching them splash around in the shallows near the bank.

She didn't know why they popped into her head

at that moment. It almost made her giggle, and the thought of that pleased her even more. She kicked her legs out again. The thrust of it was a bit too zealous. Her shoulder hit the slimy wall of the tunnel, reminding her that she wasn't in Ohio anymore. Her body flinched, and she dropped the flashlight.

It didn't fall far.

The water was murky, but she could see the light, maybe two or three feet below her. She squinted at it. Yes, it was the flashlight and it was within her reach.

A splash broke her concentration. It was distant, but distinct and not of her own making. She gulped a lungful of musty air, and dove back under the water's surface. The bottom was much closer than she had thought. Her hands scraped over the floor. Her fingertips grazed the flashlight, and sent it rolling. The light bounced through the depths.

She frantically reached for it, but her time was gone. She needed to breathe.

Her feet pushed gently off the floor and she waved her arms to slow her ascent. The tip of her head breached the surface and she tilted it back. She sucked in the stale air.

Another splash. This time it was much louder, closer. She lowered herself back down so that her hands could continue their search of the tunnel floor. This time, Keira laid a hand directly on her prize.

She switched it off and the water around her darkened. It was too dark--too quick. She held onto her last breath. Her eyes remained open, wide open, though she couldn't see beyond the tip of her nose. The murky dark of the water wrapped around her.

Her chest began to ache as the last of her air supply dwindled. That's when she remembered the dagger strapped to her ankle.

Keira's fingers moved deftly to unlatch the weapon from its sheath. She flipped up the securing band just as something jerked her forward.

It had latched onto her right shoulder. She scratched at it, but it held tight.

Another tug. Her feet scrambled under her. She took in more of the nasty water.

Another tug. The water became shallow. She could touch the bottom. She bent her knees and sprang up. Her attacker fell over into the water. She tried to run, but the water and her drenched clothing kept her to a slowed pace.

"Keira, wait!" she heard him cry out.

Him. Not a mogdoc. Him. There was only one *him* in the Citadel.

Keira stopped, holding her dagger at the ready, hidden close to her side. Brun didn't take his eyes off her as he stood. Although she could not see him, she knew. She could feel his eyes on her. She was glad she couldn't see him in the darkness. The sight of him made her too angry.

She took a step back toward him. The next step was much quicker than the first. Then another and another came. When she reached him, he was on his feet. She pushed him against the tunnel wall.

"Where is my charge, mogdoc?"

"He's safe."

"So you did take him?"

He grimaced, but didn't try to move free from where she had him pinned to the slimy cavern wall. His eyes smoothed past her and over the water. She used to think that shy look to the ground, his signature move, was cute. Now, she couldn't help but think that it was fake, just another tool in his manipulation arsenal. It probably took a lot of time to perfect, but she was sure that it was time well spent. No doubt many girls had agreed to many things after being delivered that look from his smoldering, green eyes.

The thought of it infuriated her even more. She took hold of his chin and pulled his focus back to her.

"Did you take him?"

He closed his eyes and nodded.

"Ahhhgg," her disappointment bellowed in a guttural roar. Clearly appalled, her hands opened as she stepped back.

"He's fine. He's safe," Brun rushed to explain.

"He better be. Where is he?"

"You don't understand."

"I don't. I don't understand how you could possibly believe that I would ever trust you. You took him from me."

"Now, Keira..."

"Oh, don't you dare. Don't. You. Dare. I'm not playing your game anymore. Tell me where he is or I'll take out everyone upstairs to find him."

"Keep your voice down," he insisted through clenched teeth. "He's not here. I told you. He's safe, out of the reach of the mogdocs, out of the reach of the Unionists, out of the reach of Elsted. All want him. I did this for you. You have to trust me."

Keira's critical eyes searched him. "You didn't do this for me."

"Of course I did. What could I possibly have to gain?" the anger rose in his voice as he spoke.

Keira grabbed up the fabric of his shirt at the shoulders. She tightened her grip on him and her resolve with it. She leaned in close...close enough to feel his warm breath on her forehead. Beads of water ran down her arms and escaped at the elbows. She didn't bother to move the strands of wet hair that plastered her face.

"If you ever felt anything for me," she said, breathing hard. "Tell me where you're keeping him. He's my responsibility. He's tied to me. I have to protect him."

"And I have to protect..."

Keira fell to her knees and covered her ears as a siren blared from its spot on the ceiling. Brun took her arm and pulled her through the water as he ran. His hand felt warm on her cold, wet skin. A little farther and the water became shallower and shallower until it ended onto a dirt and stone floor. The shrill of the alarms grew louder which could only mean one thing. They were moving toward the heart of the Citadel.

The tunnel narrowed as they went. Soon it became so small that they would have to crawl to continue. Wordlessly, Brun moved behind Keira. She didn't like that. She couldn't see him. She would have to trust him; there was no choice.

It was impossible to hold a flashlight or even her dagger while crawling. She placed the dagger back in its ankle sheath for safekeeping. She stuffed the flashlight handle in her back pocket as far as it would go. Instead, Keira depended on her sense of touch to lead her through. She edged her way slowly, and knew that Brun was following close behind. After a long while, the tunnel opened up enough so that they could stand again. Brun wedged himself beside her and mouthed directions which she couldn't understand.

She shook her head. The sirens were too loud. The tunnel was too dark.

His flattened hand rose between them. She knew what that meant, even if she didn't want to. Wait.

Then, Brun's head flew around to the subtle, yet unmistakable, sound of footsteps. Keira heard it too, if just for a second between the unceasing bellows of the alarm. She stepped, careful to keep low so as not to hit her head on the ceiling. She scanned the darkened room. Her fingers slide over her flashlight, but she didn't turn it on.

Brun touched her shoulder, and then placed a finger in front of his pursed lips. She watched him silently as his hand fell from her shoulder. He eased away from her along the stone wall. Her eyes stayed on him until he vanished into the darkness.

And then he was gone. Her stomach left its proper place too, and replacing it was a sinking feeling.

Alone in the dark, Keira's hand traveled down her jeans to her ankle. The sirens stopped abruptly as she grasped the handle of her dagger. It seemed a coincidence, but it couldn't have been. She didn't even get it out of the sheath before a hand clamped over her mouth. The other arm reached around her stomach and pulled her fully upright.

"Shhh. We've got to get you out of here. This way," Brun whispered, removing his hand from her mouth. The other held firm over her midriff. His cheek prickled her ear as his mouth opened. "They're coming."

She moved her head to the side so she could see his face. "I told you," she whispered back. "I'm not going without Drew."

"This way," he urged again.

She couldn't see, but he held her hand. They ran

through an offshoot of the tunnel, twisting and turning until it finally opened up into a grand room.

Brun lit a torch in the corner. The light reflected off a lake that took up most of the cavern. Keira gasped.

"You recognize it, don't you?"

She did. The lake, the sand and mud, and the cavern with its dripping stalactites were a permanent fixture in her nightmares. Every detail of them etched in her mind for good.

This was where she plunged her poisoned dagger into Emperor Gammen's black heart. This was where Brun's father then died. And though she would do it again if given the chance, a rogue tear tumbled down her cheek.

Before she could say a word or even take a breath, Brun swept her up in his arms and kissed her. His lips were soft and unrushed, despite the circumstance. She remembered kissing him like this long ago when they were boyfriend and girlfriend, just two kids who bumped into each other at a pep assembly at school.

Times had changed since then. She forced herself to remember. There was a reason why she was standing in a cavern deep under the mogdoc Citadel.

She pushed at his chest. He tightened his arms around her and pulled her back in. Her hand flew out to the side and landed across his cheek.

"You shouldn't have come here," he breathed. The side of his face was already turning red. "These caves are sacred to my people."

He staggered back from her and pulled a single finger down, following an invisible line known only to him. When he finished, the mogdoc threshold glowed in the air like a crooked seam of light.

She wiped her mouth with her hand incredulously.

“Take me to Drew.”

"You don't understand. The Sect is searching the Citadel for intruders. I won't be able . . . if they find you . . ."

"Don't give me that," she waved her hand in the air. "We're in some kind of secret cavern. I'll bet they don't even know about this place."

"Are you willing to bet your life on that?" he whispered. "Go, I never meant to keep him. Meet me at the Landing at noon tomorrow, and I'll lead you right to him."

"Take me to him now."

His eyes shot down the adjoining tunnel, and then back to her. He still had an arm wrapped around her center, which he nervously shifted. He was so close; she could feel his heartbeat. Rapid. Anxious. She knew it was more than he could fake.

"Now," she pushed.

He shook his head. "You have to go without me," he pleaded. "I'll be there tomorrow. It will look too suspicious if I disappear now, and you can't stay. I can't protect you here. They barely even listen to *her* anymore and I'm worse...less..."

But Keira wasn't listening. She sidestepped then pivoted, using her leverage and his surprise to throw him off balance and push him through the threshold ahead of her.

* * *

Grass. Sun. Earth. He kicked his feet furiously

and dug his nails into the ground. "Keira!" he screamed from her backyard.

Keira had used her momentum to break away as soon as they touched ground. She crouched on her knees, ready to spring at him with dagger in hand just in case.

"Pray that wasn't the mistake of your life," he grunted.

"You brought this on yourself. Now, take me to Drew."

He took his time standing up, periodically peering at her from the corner of his eye. Impatience swelled in her as he dusted the freshly cut grass and dirt from his jeans. His green eyes, more human than mogdoc, reflected brightly as they adjusted to the sunlight. She watched him carefully and the more she did so, the more her stomach turned.

Because he looked like just a boy.

He looked like the star running back at Valley View High. He looked like the boy that noticed her at her locker. He looked like the boy who bought her a strawberry milkshake on their first date.

He looked like the boy who just got her out of the Citadel alive.

Keira focused on her hands and tried to center herself. Time for a reality check. He *was* the boy who kidnapped her charge. She gulped and tightened her grip on her dagger.

When she looked up again, he was standing right in front of her, hands out and a blank look on his face. "You comin'?"

She nodded and took up beside him.

Keira let him lead the way into the field. This time, Colby's father, Curt, had planted soybeans. Not that anyone would know that at this early stage. Their green leaves peeked out just above the surface. Keira walked carefully so as not to extinguish the new life; while Brun paid the budding plants no such respect.

"Where are we going?" Keira asked. "Can't you just open the threshold right here?"

"The walk will do you good," he said, without as much as a look her way.

He took a right into the tall grasses of the hay field. They tromped through the middle, the grasses bowing down at their footfalls. Over the hill, next to a line of trees, Keira could make out something red. Brun's strides became longer as it came into view. Keira's sigh bundled regret and relief. The early rays of dawn revealed a red, four-door pickup.

It wasn't Brun's truck. It was William's, the boy he pretended to be once upon a time.

"What's your truck doing here?" she asked to which he just shrugged. It only took a few more steps for her to piece it together. "He's on this side of the barrier?"

"I'm protecting him from the things across the barrier, remember? Do you think I would keep him in the Citadel?"

"Just so we're clear," she said as she jumped into the cab. "You *kidnapped* him from me, his true guardian. You know, the one who is bound by duty to protect him."

"I had no choice."

"So what? Is kidnapping like a mogdoc graduation project?"

"Midnight child or not, that kid is important. If he is your charge, he's probably the gift from the prophecy. If he's just a midnight child, then he's a distraction from our child, who'll be the true gift."

"I'm not going to listen to this nonsense again," she grimaced.

"Fine." He slid his hands around the steering wheel before starting up the engine. "I wish..."

Keira talked to the passenger side window. "I'm not in the wish-granting mood today. And don't think that this time together changes anything. I know where you really stand. I won't make that mistake again."

"What mistake?"

"Trusting you."

He sighed deeply. Neither of them breathed another word as the moments passed. Brun's eyes glanced over at the right side mirror from time to time, but never directly at Keira. Keira sat quietly, staring ahead, trying to ascertain their final destination.

It was hard. Harder than one might think. She found her mind drifting, playing on times not so long ago. The truck teased her with its smells of leather and diesel fuel. Smells that brought her back to the fall they spent together as boyfriend and girlfriend.

Finally, Brun was the first to break the silence.

"You know, it's not nonsense, you and I."

"It's not going to happen."

"Because you can't accept what I am?"

She rolled her eyes. "What you are right now is the jerk who stole a little kid from his parents."

"You are so thick!" he growled in frustration. "You are mine. I did this for you. Charge or midnight child, regardless of *what* Drew is, he is power. He's the leverage that everyone wants."

"Like you?"

"Like the Sect of Low."

Keira knew the Sect of Low. They were the

mogdoc crown's elite assassins, known to be lightning quick and vicious.

“What could they possibly want with a toddler? she asked in disbelief.

"Forget it," Brun shook his head. "I shouldn't have said anything. You're just...trying to get through to you is... just...just...completely frustrating."

"You want me to trust you. Then tell me what you know."

"I know Broo's losing control," he continued after he made another turn. "She's off her game. They distrust her. It doesn't take much. Mogdocs aren't an exceptionally loyal bunch."

"And they need Drew for what exactly?"

“They don’t know. They just know that he’s important and therefore must be controlled.”

“But you know, don’t you?” she asked, her eyes unrelenting.

"We're here," Brun said, ignoring Keira's question completely.

She looked out the window, and reprimanded herself for not thinking to check the house before. From her passenger's side window she could see water flowing from the angry Poseidon fountain in the center of the drive. This was Broo's house when she infiltrated the life of a teenager and posed as cheerleader Brooke Banes.

Brun jumped from the truck and slammed the door behind. Keira scanned the back for weapons. There were none. She didn't think there would be, but it was worth a quick check.

There was nothing in the seat but a supply of fresh, long-stemmed red roses…of course. He had been leaving them everywhere for her to find. If invited, it would have been a grand romantic gesture. Yeah, well, she wasn't into grand romantic gestures. She fought down the urge to chuck them out the window.

Brun ducked back in. "Hold up. I'm gonna move to the back."

Keira watched him as he started the truck and shifted into gear. As soon as they were moving, he stretched an arm over the top of the bench seat. He eased the truck over the curb of the driveway and into the grass. They circled behind the main house to a smaller structure behind.

At first glance, Keira thought it to be a pool house. She had never actually seen one before except in a magazine and certainly not in their small town. However, this was not a pool house. It was much too modest and too closed-in for that. The smallish, plain building before them was once servants' quarters.

The truck came to a halt at the front door. Brun wasn't looking at the building. He was staring at the steering wheel.

"She'll use the shadows to re-invoke the Harvest. Once she does that, she will be unstoppable."

"She? You mean Broo?"

He nodded. "Keira, you weren't wrong. I do know why they need Drew."

"And you are going to use him to take your sister's place."

"Don't put words in my mouth. I took him to protect him. I never lied to you about that. They know he's important. What they don't know," Brun sighed, "is that your charge can control the shadows. The creatures are drawn to him. He moves a hand and they jump to attention. I've never seen anything like it. His effect on them must be his contribution to the world. It's why he's special."

Brun jumped out before the engine made its final clunk. Keira scrambled to undo her seatbelt under the brick on information he lofted onto her lap. She followed him to the front door. Brun bowed slightly and waved an "after you" gesture.

Too late, the thought that this could be a trap fluttered through her mind.

He caught her eyes, and immediately knew what she was thinking. "I'll go first," he whispered sadly.

He opened the door and though she was behind him, Keira could hear the smile instantly appear in his voice.

"I brought a surprise for you, big boy!"

"Kiki! Kiki!"

Keira's breath caught and she couldn't get around Brun fast enough. Drew jumped into her arms. She pulled his head to her chest and held him tightly. She closed her eyes and mouthed, "Thank you."

"And now, the rat's here? What are you thinking?" a shrill voice, dripping with ice, griped.

Keira eyes targeted her. She had been so focused on Drew, too focused. Alexa Banes stood, hands on hips, in front of them. Her slick, black tailored suit and dripping jewels seemed wildly out of place in the humble servants' quarters.

"Quiet, please," Brun requested half-heartedly.

"Son, you had the boy. No one could stop you. We were perfectly positioned to regain our rightful place in the Empire. Are you really going to let her walk away with him?" Alexa spit back.

"That's up to her."

And with that, all eyes were on Keira.

She steadied her dagger in one hand and held on to Drew ever tightly with the other. He clung to her just as tightly. "I'm taking him with me. Do not try to stop me."

"Keira, listen to me because this is the last time I'm going to try to explain," he reached for her hand.

Keira's defense was quick and smooth, a result of her training. A line of crimson burst from his palm. He grasped his wrist and wrenched the pain away. Keira stood shocked by her own action. Her heart beat solidly in her chest, matched by Drew's against it.

"Keira, the Sect was coming after him. I took him into custody to *protect* him, to teach him how to use his gift. You have to believe me."

Brun took another step, and so did she. “I’m sorry,” she mouthed, shaking her head furiously, “Just stay back.”

She lifted her dagger slightly higher. He had to know that she would slice him again, even though she was not sure herself, if she could.

"They don't know it was me," he said. "They think you are behind his disappearance; that you detected their plans somehow. Their paranoia will be enough to deter them from another attempt at least for now. So, yes, take him back to his parents. He should be perfectly safe. I will not stand in your way. Not ever."

Keira couldn't take her eyes off him, but it wasn't his hand, it was his eyes, his green mogdoc eyes. Drew began to cry into her shoulder. She absentmindedly rocked him.

Then she stopped.

"Take him!" she screamed.

Brun grabbed hold of the child just before Keira

disappeared.

Chapter 7: The Unfortunate Rescue

Flat on her back, Keira looked up. Her friends surrounded her.

"What?!? You?" she shouted.

She started to get up, but realized she wasn't on the ground. It was too hard to be the ground, besides she was lying at waist-level to her friends.

Colby pulled his "old man" bald cap and fake nose off as he explained, "Things were too hot. Katie pulled us all out. We're at The Landing."

It was usually her favorite spot to watch the sunset; however, this day she would watch it rise. The morning dew left its moisture on the picnic tables in the shelterhouse. Keira didn't let it bother her as she lay on the one that was usually her favorite, the table directly in the shelter's center.

"Sorry?" Katie's shoulders rose and fell with her

face. "I freaked when we all got split up. That was too intense."

"You did well," Ann said, putting her arm around her sister. "Don't doubt yourself. We put a traveler's mark on everyone so you or I could get everyone to safety if things went wrong."

"I thought that's why you *had* to have the coins?" Mikey broke in, sitting at a picnic table a few feet away. She looked more than a little bored.

Ann replied, "The mark is just something for us to target our ability to pull someone back to this side. That person still has to have a token to cross the barrier."

"How do ya'll live with all these rules? Glad I'm a wolf."

Jumper put his hand up in the air. "Um, just wanted to point out that the ordinary humans in the group pulled off their assignment without a hitch."

Colby started to laugh, but Keira’s glare stopped him.

"You saw Brun?" Ann asked.

"I saw him," Katie chimed in. "He is still so hot. He got me out."

"What do you mean, he got you out?" Keira asked.

"Well, Annie told me to run. I did and practically ran into him. He distracted the guards and told me how to get out. Once I was out, I went straight to the rendezvous point. After, like forever, no one else showed up. That's when I panicked and pulled everyone back here."

"You saw him too?" Keira asked Ann.

"Apparently after he showed Katie the exit."

"Busy guy," Jumper said, just as Colby's phone

buzzed in his pocket.

"You don't know the half of it," Keira said. "He did it, you know."

Ann squinted. "We don't for sure if he's the one that kidnapped Drew."

"Now we do," Keira said. "Come on."

"But why?" Ann asked. "Why would he take Drew? It just doesn't make sense."

"I had Drew in my hands," Keira said to everyone's shock. "Just before you pulled me back. He's at Broo's old house on Main. Let's go get him."

"Wait," Colby said with hand raised and the phone to his ear.

Mikey humphed, "You gotta be kidding me. I was so up for a fight."

Keira narrowed her eyes at Mikey, but she just shrugged them off. The conversation to which her werewolf hearing made her privy was much more urgent.

Colby ended the call and proceeded to explain to the group what he and the werewolf already knew. The police found Drew. Well, "found" would imply that it was the result of searching, which was not the case. Just moments before, an officer nearly stumbled over Drew whom had been left on the steps outside the police station.

* * *

That night, Keira paced the floor of her room. She wasn't one for pacing. She supposed Arden's constant habit had rubbed off on her somehow. Arden was the master of pacing, if there was a trophy or a black belt for it, it was probably hanging on a shelf in his bedroom.

Keira knew what Arden would say now:

She should know
that thinking about Brun was wrong.

She should know
that it was a bad idea to contact him.

She should know
that this was all part of some master seduction.

However, she didn't know any of those things. Not really.

The concerned shape of Brun's mouth as he told her that her charge could control the shadows echoed in her mind.

Keira had asked her mother about the shadows. It wasn't a surprise that Bianca didn't want to talk about them. She was nearly killed by them when she was Keira's age. They covered her mouth and nose, and when she fell into unconsciousness they dragged her body through the woods to the Emperor's feet. Only her fierce survival instinct saved her that night. Bianca was now forever the *Girl Who Got Away.* Her escape recounted over and over as a cautionary bedtime story for guardian children.

Keira stopped pacing as she reached the window. *Do it*, she willed herself.

She threw open the sash and slipped out, just as she had a few times before. Usually those stolen moments were spent on visits to see her best friend, Colby. No matter the problem, he was always a source of comfort. Tonight she would go to Colby's house, but it wasn't to visit him. Deep inside, she couldn't ignore the feeling that someone else would be there.

The night was warm, even though a slight breeze stirred. She made her way through the soybean field. She knew the way over the uneven path, even if she couldn't see. That was nearly the case as clouds worked to block out the moon and stars. The air was thick; the kind that always preceded the summer rain.

As the dirt started to dimple here and there, her steps came quicker. Cool drops chilled her shoulders left bare by her tank top. Steps turned into a jog as the two-story farmhouse came into sight. If she ran hard enough, she could reach his porch before the downpour.

In seconds, she covered the yard. Just a few strides more would land her on the steps and she could wait out the rain on the porch.

Maybe that's why it happened. She was so focused on escaping the rain. Her sneaker slid on the wet grass. Arms circled wildly over her head, eager to find balance or support. They landed on clean, soft cloth. Her feet skittered beneath her as the man under the white robe grabbed her hair and pulled her head back.

"The guardian," a whisper rose and echoed among the small group. "The guardian," their murmurs above the tumbles of the strengthening rain. "The guardian."

Hands flew to her sides, and held her arms out. She pulled against them, but there were too many. "Let me go," she screamed.

Immediately, they let go. She hadn't expected it and fell on her knees.

"We wish you no harm, guardian. We have come

for the midnight child. Trust that this is for the best," a tall man said. His mouth barely moved, unmarked by expression or emotion of any kind.

Rain began to pour over them. Keira scanned the group to etch every face into her memory; two eager young men, perhaps twins, with strong chins and light coloring; a plump, young woman with red curls falling out of her hooded cloak; a buxom brunette with a permanent sneer; and a mustached brute with a nasty scar through his left eyebrow.

Then, her eyes flickered back to the leader, a bald man with soulless black eyes. Him she knew. It had taken her only a moment to realize he was the one that crashed Jumper's last Halloween party. He had come for her charge that night too.

"You know that I will never allow you to take him."

"Your loyalty is misplaced with the Hayes family," the bald man answered with a voice that chilled her to the bone. "Allow us to remove the distraction so that you may fulfill your true destiny."

"He is *not* a midnight child. He is my charge."

"He is of no consequence."

A crack sounded, causing everyone to look up. A dark figure stood on the edge of the roof. He stepped forward and landed softly on the ground. He stood tall beside Keira.

Brun's voice was heavy with anger. "You heard her. The child is not to be touched."

"But…" the leader of the group started.

His dispute was not heard because Brun was behind him in the next second. The shine of Brun's short sword glistened at the man's ear.

"If you will not listen, perhaps you do not need

this ear," Brun growled. "From this day forward, let it be known that the guardian and I *both* protect this child. Whoever dares to approach him will succumb to the full wrath of the Empire *and* Elsted. You will leave now…ahhh!"

The leader wrenched his dagger out of Brun's side. Blood dripped from the dagger's edge. Brun stumbled back, his face a mixture of disbelief and horror.

"What have you done?" one of the Unionist girls screamed as Brun dropped to his knees.

Keira used the distraction to disarm the red head. Her knife was long and of good weight. Keira took it straight to the leader's throat.

"No need for rash action. He will heal. He will still be of use to you," the man's voice remained steady, though the tip of the sword depressed the thin layer of skin covering his Adam's apple.

"Oh, so not the point," Keira said. "You keep yapping about my charge being a distraction, but here I am dealing with you again. Leave us and my charge alone or die tonight at my hand. I mean it, jerk wad."

The leader took a generous step back and she allowed it.

"It appears that things are well in hand," he said slyly. "You have my word that we will take our leave and not return, unless on your command. If you, my queen, should need our services, we are at the ready. Forward to the Fall."

"Forward to the Fall," the others echoed.

Keira lowered to help Brun up. Neither one looked to the other; instead, their eyes followed the white robes as they backed away toward the river, rolling like a white fog.

When the intruders were finally gone, Brun exhaled unsteadily and bobbled where he stood. His sword still in hand, he used his forearm to wipe the water from his pale face. "That was unfortunate," he choked.

"Yeah," she breathed. "We need to get you out of the rain."

Keira shouldered Brun as they made their way to the nearby barn. She slid the heavy door open with little effort. It rumbled as it rolled along its track. Inside the barn, it was completely dry; tucked away from the night's rain. Yet, Keira could still hear the tapping chorus of raindrops on the metal roof.

She flipped on the lights. They hummed as they gradually reached their maximum brilliance. Their light splashed over stacks and stacks of square hay bales bound of sweet alfalfa and clover.

Brun was steady enough to stand on his own. Barely. She left him momentarily to retrieve a blanket stashed in the cab of the tractor. She knew it would be there. Curt Hayes always had one for little ones that joined him to take a ride, like she and Colby when they were younger and now for his grandson, Drew.

As soon as the blanket settled on the ground, Brun collapsed onto it. The crocheted yarn in hues of green and yellow was soft to the touch, but smelled of dust and diesel fuel. His stomach twinged from the scent; forcing him to let out a breath he didn't know he was holding.

"Does it hurt?" Keira gasped, immediately wishing she hadn't. Truth be told, she didn't know what to say, what to do. She had seen him hurt before, but not like this. His defenses lowered. Pain so visibly etched on his face. "Sorry, of course it does."

With one hand pressed against the wound, he used the other to carefully remove his shirt. Before it cleared his head, she put a hand on his side. His muscles tensed at her touch. He looked up and was surprised to see fear in her brown eyes.

"Like he said, I'll heal. It's no worse than the times *you* stabbed me." He teased, though it was strained. "I just need to sit and rest for a little while."

He put his hand on hers and brushed it away.

Worry wrinkled her forehead. "We should go to the hospital. I can go get Mom's car and pull it right up to the barn door."

"And just how are you going to explain my blood type? How are you going to explain the coin in my arm if they take an x-ray? My black…" he winced.

"Right. No human doctors," she said.

She wouldn't make him admit it because she already suspected what beat inside his chest. It was common knowledge to those that were other than human. Poetic justice or a cosmic joke; regardless, it was a universal truth. Mogdocs literally have black hearts.

Keira stepped from the blanket and rummaged around on a nearby workbench for a time. Soon she returned and lowered herself on her knees, an army green first aid kit in her hands.

"Let me see," she said, making quick work of the latch.

Her face was serious, determined. He didn't brush her away this time. The heat of his skin now softened under her touch. The cut wasn't wide, but it looked deep. Dried blood caked in and around the point of entry. She removed a small bottle of disinfectant and some gauze, and proceeded to clean.

"Do you heal fast?" she asked. "Supernaturally fast, like me?"

He shook his head, but she didn't see it. All her attention was focused on his wounded side. Realizing that she was still waiting for an answer, he finally whispered, "No."

She looked up. She was close, really close, just inches from his lips. He was breathing hard, and to her surprise, she was too.

"Right…then we'll have to stitch this up," she swallowed. "I just wish Ann was here. She's always good in an emergency."

"I'll do it," he said. "You don't have to."

She stopped him with a finger placed on his lips. She would have said something, explained, but all her words were gone. Her eyes sparkled on his. He put his hand on hers, and brought it down.

"Thank you."

She shook her head to clear it. "No problem."

Her fingers delved back into the first aid kit and uncovered the items she needed, a needle and a small spool of fine elastic thread. They were items that weren't part of the usual basic first aid kit, but she knew she would find them in this one. Farm work was dangerous, about as dangerous as being a guardian.

She threaded the needle expertly. Even Nana would have been impressed.

"Are you ready?" she asked.

She helped him lay back and put a hand on his stomach to steady him.

"Go on," he said when he was ready.

She sank the needle in, and started to pull the skin back together, stitch by stitch. It was easier than she thought it would be. Almost like sewing on a button.

"There's something I have to tell you about your charge," he started.

"Are you sure it's a good idea to tell me now when I have a needle in your side?"

"Better than your dagger," he smiled weakly. "Remember what I told you before—about how your charge could control the shadows?"

"Yeah?" she prompted, not sure where he was going with his.

"It was different."

"How do you mean?"

Brun thought for a moment before replying.

"He moves, they move. It's a dance. He doesn't command them by fear like the Emperor did. It's more like respect…no, admiration. They adore him. They've chosen him."

"So what happens now?"

"I don't know yet. It makes him desirable. There's not a soul in Atlantis that wouldn't kill to control the one that controls the shadows. You need to guard his ability, keep it secret."

She seemed to consider that for a long moment. He watched her work silently to keep the stitches even, and when she was done, he cut the thread.

"Nice work," he said. "Thank you. I'm feeling better already."

"Mogdocs lie," she teased.

It was the first time he found amusement in the statement. One corner of her mouth curved up as she knotted the end.

"What?"

"Nothing really," she said, placing a bandage over her work. I was just thinking about the time I stabbed you. I couldn't see and I thought you were attacking me. You remember? That was when I let Broo's soldiers capture me so that I could get in the Citadel. Your rebels ambushed them in the woods. Boy that was…"

"Two years ago," he finished for her. "It does seem to happen a lot when you're around."

"Not a lot. Just the once. Oh wait, no, there was that other time," she said with a hint of guilt this time. "The second was when I stabbed you on the beach. You had plucked me right off the stairs at the hospital, kept me from Colby, and I fell into the water. Ah, I was raging. Furious. I've never been so mad in my life. And then, you…"

"I tried to kiss you," he whispered. "You were so angry, but so full of passion, so beautiful…I hold that memory with me."

She pulled her head back to see his expression packed with sadness and regret. Fat raindrops on the metal roof ticked away the seconds. He leaned in closer. His woodsy scent, crisp as the midnight forests of Atlantis, filled her head. She tried to remember to breathe.

Keira brushed a hand through her hair and looked around. Nervous energy flooded her body. Her hands wanted to be busy. She twisted her fingers in her hair and suddenly realized that it was still wet. In fact, she was still completely drenched.

Keira had rushed out her open window in nothing but a pair of sneakers, shorts, and a tank top. All now soaked from the rain. Brun gave a small grunt of disapproval as she left the blanket. On the workbench, she found a small space heater and one of Curt's old flannel work shirts. She quickly put them to use.

Within ten minutes, her hair was drying nicely.

Her shoes were lined up neatly in front of the heater. She didn't strip down. She wasn't that fearless or insane. Instead, she pulled the flannel shirt over her wet clothes and buttoned it up to her chin. It helped. She felt safe and warm, and then the mogdoc spoke.

"Sit with me," Brun said reaching a hand out to her.

She bit her lip. Seeing her hesitation, he pulled his hand back to the bandage on his side. His mind searched for a distraction.

"It didn't sound like they would come back," Brun said to the rafters of the barn.

"They were wearing Unionists' robes," she added.

"They were trying to get to Colby again or maybe they found out about Drew," Brun confirmed. "I'm not really sure, but I'm glad that we didn't let it get far enough to find out."

"Thanks for helping me out back there." She stepped onto the blanket and lowered herself to sit cross-legged.

"Yeah, well, it didn't go exactly as I'd planned when I stepped off the roof. My plan was more about being the hero and less about being the comic relief."

Keira smiled. "You started out strong, swooping down like an avenging angel with all that wrath of the Empire stuff."

The glance he gave her was incredulous. "You thought I looked like an angel?"

"You just need to work on the closing."

He laughed, abruptly stopped by a shooting pain. The corners of Keira's mouth drooped.

"No, no. Don't get quiet on me. Let's keep talking," he said. "It helps not to think about it."

"Okay. Let's see. So the Unionists, they were the same group that was here before…last Halloween."

"That's right. The big one who did all the talking is called Gawain. Tough guy. Kind of guy that lines his closet with mogdoc skin boots, a pair for every day of the month."

"I thought the Unionists…"

"Liked me? Followed me? Worshipped me? Common misconception. Believe me, they don't. They're looking for the end of my family's rule, the 'fall of the House of Gammen'. It really tugs at their panties that they need me to do it."

"Huh," Keira whispered curtly.

The conversation was quickly getting into dangerous territory. And sure enough his next words were, "The Unionists and me, there's only one thing we agree on."

His eyes wouldn't move from hers, yet she couldn't look at him.

"Is it so terrible?" he asked. He pulled his elbows back to prop himself up. He wanted to see her face when she answered.

"Being stripped of my own decisions? Yes, Brun, it sucks."

"No, Keira, I meant...am *I* so terrible?"

Before her, that question didn't even exist in his mind where the opposite sex was concerned. Now, it wouldn't leave.

"Am I so terrible that you won't even consider a life with me? Do you have any idea how many girls would do anything to have me say that they are mine?"

Her eyes narrowed on him, "Guess I'm not like the sluts you typically hang with."

He breathed heavily. “No, there’s no one. That’s not what I meant. I…”

“Stop,” she pushed her hair over her shoulder and her anger with it. “I know what you meant, and no, you’re not terrible.”

“At least I don’t think so,” she continued. “You saved my life…more than once. Every time I think you’re doing wrong…somehow…it turns out right. But…”

“But?”

“But you should be,” her chest fell. “You are a mogdoc. You should be terrible. And I know that all this is probably just camouflage.”

“Can I kiss you?”

“Can do what?” she stumbled over the words, shaking her head like she didn’t understand.

He smiled a slight smile, just enough to trigger his dimples. His eyes poured over the blanket shyly. She had seen him give that shy look dozens of times. It was one of the things that she found so attractive about him when she saw him for the first time at school. Strange how a movement so minute could be so familiar, so comforting.

“Can I…” he started again to ask for permission, which was certainly something he wasn’t used to doing, but he didn’t have to. Her lips met his. Her fingers smoothed over the short hair on the back of his neck, pulling her down to him.

His strong jaw yielded to her. The kisses came constant, restless; each more eager and intense than the last. A low groan escaped his throat sending chills through her body. She felt herself drift away. His hands roamed under the flannel shirt, down her back, gripped her waist, and pushed her away.

“I’m sorry,” he huffed as the room spun around him. His face flushed. “I’m sorry. Ahh, forget it.”

He pulled her back to his lips, but it was short lived. He groaned again, and she realized it was caused by pain, not pleasure. She could see red flood his bandages. It was enough to bring her back to the real world.

Keira cleaned his wound a second time and replaced his bandages. Fatigue finally overwhelmed Brun halfway through the process. He fell asleep before she was finished.

Keira’s eyes weren’t on the first aid box as she closed it. They looked upon the mogdoc prince as he stirred and nestled more deeply into the green and yellow afghan.

She couldn’t help but think that he looked just like a boy.

But he wasn’t.

He never would be.

She returned the box to the work bench, picked up her shoes, slipped out of the barn, and headed for home.

Chapter 8: Backyard Surveillance

Colby made his way across the backyard, cradling a couple cans of soda in the crook of his arm as he balanced a bowl of popcorn in his hands. A sliver of the moon lit up the path to Keira's tent.

His parents had thought it cute at first; Colby and Keira camping out in the backyard like they did when they were little. However, a night turned into a week, which turned into a month, which led to the entire summer.

"Just what are you doing out there every night," his Dad demanded.

"Nothing's going on," Colby would always say. "Don't believe me, just drop in. You'll see."

"What does her father have to say about it?"

"He approves; likes that she's taking advantage of summer, getting fresh air, and all of that," Colby would reply.

"A boy your age shouldn't be alone all night with

a girl. Even if it is just Keira," Curt returned.

Then Lila, who always seemed to take up for Colby's side, would convince Curt that he was overreacting, and nothing more would be made of it until a few more nights passed. At that point, the conversation would recycle, always ending with the same inaction. Colby knew, though, that his days were numbered. The tolerated summer nights would soon come to an end with the start of school.

When Colby reached the tent, he found the door zipped shut. He tried to juggle the snacks to free a hand. One of the colas slipped from his grasp and tumbled toward the ground. A hand caught it just before impact.

Colby jumped at her sudden presence. "You've got to stop doing that."

Keira shrugged and popped open the tab. The can foamed up. She let the excess roll off its edge and onto the ground before slipping into the tent.

"Just made the rounds," she said. "Looks like another quiet night."

"The last night," he reminded her. "Senior year starts day after tomorrow. This is the last night in the tent. You'll have to figure out some other way to watch over Drew."

"Actually, I've been thinkin' about that. We should have called it quits a few weeks ago," she admitted. "It doesn't look like they are going to come for him. They would have struck long before now."

Colby agreed, but didn't voice it. He just listened. He was good at listening.

"The Unionists are in front of the Elders every day. They don't have time to plan anything else, and they don't have to. It's working. Dad says they've gained the ears of at least a couple of members."

And so there are also times when listening isn't enough.

"They're actually buying that load of bull," he fumed. "You and Brun, like an arranged marriage or something? They can't do that."

"Probably not," she mumbled before gulping her soda.

"*Probably* not! That's not good enough. I'm sure that there must be some guardian law that protects you. We'll go to the library in Elsted and research it. We can…"

"Yeah, well," she interrupted. "I'm sure you're aching to crack open some dusty old law book, but don't sweat it. You know the Council. They move like snails on a salt trail. Besides, I think the Sect of Low will take action long before that happens. Brun says…"

"*Brun* says? Oh yeah, what does Brun say about all this, because I'm just dying to know what Brun thinks," Colby said, his words coated with an extra thick layer of sarcasm.

"Don't be that way. If you don't want to hear it," she tempted as she shifted her attention out a side opening so that she could keep watch on Drew's bedroom window.

It wasn't as if he had a reason to be jealous, she thought. She hadn't touched Brun since that rainy night in the barn. Their interactions these days were infrequent and awkward. Everything was at stake. She couldn't afford the risk of getting caught up in the moment again. Not when it came to Brun.

"Fine. What did your mogdoc stalker have to say?"

She swatted at him and he pretended to be offended.

"Anyway, *Brun* thinks that the Sect is going to throw your old girlfriend under the bus."

"That makes zero sense."

"Did you honestly think that the most evil, vicious creatures alive would blindly follow the cheerleader captain?"

"When you put it that way," he smirked. "But we both know that's not all she is."

"Exactly," Keira said. "She may be Gammen's daughter, but she's part human too. According to Brun, she hasn't been too careful about concealing that fact. Broo rarely takes her mogdoc form these days. It's making the members of the Sect very uneasy."

The gears in his head turned, remembering the times he had seen Broo since she became Empress. He remembered when he found her in his room on the day of her coronation. She wanted to know that he was safe. She wanted to know if he missed her.

Then again she appeared to him after Drew had been taken to let him know that his nephew was safe. She warned him about Brun, and he accused her of caring. That night he noticed the necklace he gave her. It was still dangling from her neck.

"I'll take the first shift," Colby offered. It would be easy to stay awake. As always, he had a lot of thinking to do.

"Thanks," she said.

She looked at him, his golden hair perfect as always, cropped close to his scalp. His white t-shirt matched his perfectly straight, white smile. The t-shirt itself appeared to be freshly pressed, maybe even his jeans were too. That wouldn't surprise her.

Everything she lacked was everything he was. He had already kicked off his shoes and was settling into his sleeping bag. He didn't see as she touched her lips mindlessly. Once upon a time when she kissed him it felt natural like nestling into bed after a long day.

Giving her heart to him made sense. Certainly more sense than throwing her love away on Brun, who would undoubtedly end up using her in the end. She didn't want to have feelings for Brun. Maybe Colby could save her from them if she would just let him.

She wondered if she had ever really given Colby a chance. Was she the reason why it didn't work before? Did she hold back?

Here he was. There for her again, in a long list of agains. More agains than she could remember, starting with the fact that he'd wasted all summer in this tent with her. If ever there was a moment she would steal a kiss from Colby, this would be it.

"Stay focused. No sneakin' out to pick up quarters and teeth," he snorted before rolling over in his sleeping bag.

And the moment was gone.

Chapter 9: First Day of the Last Year

The next morning, Colby and Keira packed up the tent as they said goodbye to summer. The day was spent doing summer things; light hiking and fishing, splashing around in the river, and finally watching the sun set from the Landing. It was her way of saying thank you; a whole summer crammed into one, long day.

When the day was done, Keira said goodbye and started down the moonlit path toward home. She came in the back door to find a note from her parents, "dinner's in the microwave".

The heat stifled her appetite, usually the case in August. So she covered the plate in plastic wrap and slipped it in the fridge, exchanging it for a cold orange soda.

"Keira, is that you?" she heard her father call

from the study.

She came upon his door and peeked in. "Just got home. Good night."

"Wait a minute, sweetheart. Come in for a minute. We need to talk."

She raised an eyebrow and took another gulp of soda before plopping down on the overstuffed chair in the corner by the window. She pulled her legs up to her chest and let the chair swallow her up. Nana had spent many nights crocheting in that very chair. Keira inhaled. It still smelled like Nana, cherry blossom and almond oil lotion.

"So, what's up?" Keira asked.

He sighed, and Keira tightened all over. It's never good when a parent starts with a sigh.

"I know your life is complicated," he started and it felt very much like the understatement of the year. Keira took another swig of her soda.

August ran a nervous hand through his hair and chucked an old leather volume onto the desk. He shook his head as he sat in the chair beside Keira. "Complicated," he chuckled. "I sound like a fool. I've never felt so useless."

"You're not useless, Dad," she tried.

"But I am. My daughter is the child of sun and moon, and I have her sitting and waiting around on instruction from the Elders that is likely to never come."

For once, she was speechless. All summer long, and even before, her Dad had been beating the drum of patience.

"Something happened, didn't it?" she asked.

"Maybe," he said. "Arden has received information that the Empress may be planning to re-invoke the Harvest."

"I'm sure Curt could use the help on the farm," she teased dryly, referring to Colby's father.

"If only it were as easy as that," he raised a brow. "This Harvest is a royal tradition where the mogdoc ruler commands the shadows to collect human bodies for him to take back to feed his people."

"Dad, I know the story," Keira said, clearly distracted by the window. Every guardian child knew at least one story about the harvest...the story of Keira's mother, the G*irl Who Got Away.*

"It just doesn't make sense. It's not that I don't believe that Bov Gammen came to this side of the barrier and ordered up humans. I absolutely do. It's just that Broo's generation was the first that could pull others across the barrier. Her father didn't have the power to take humans across without tokens for each one."

"Keira," August said, pinching the top of his nose. "He didn't take humans across…"

She looked at him quizzically.

"…he took bodies."

"Ohhh…ewww," Keira realized a little too late.

Clothing, weapons, even flashlights–unlike living creatures, carried objects crossed the barrier just fine. The Harvest wasn't about transporting people; it was about transporting food.

The Emperor wouldn't have moved them across the barrier alive; maybe not even as whole bodies. Her stomach lurched.

She didn't realize that her father was at the door calling for her mother to join them.

Bianca Ryan stepped into the office. Her hair, a few shades darker than Keira's, was pulled into a side braid that lay softly over her shoulder. Black-framed reading glasses sat perfectly level on her tiny nose.

Over the past months, Keira had found her mother's appearance to be impeccable at all times. Even now in her evening loungewear, Bianca looked like a supermodel pretending to be a mousy librarian. It would only take removing her glasses and a tug of her braid to unleash Bianca's enormous beauty.

August shut the door behind her. Then, he took his wife's hand in his. She looked down at it and unease swept over her body as if it were a chilling wind that stirred for only her.

Soul mates, some would call them. They always knew what the other was thinking. Bianca already knew what August was going to ask of her.

Bianca took her hand back and with it, peeled her glasses from her face. "Keira," she started. "So that you *truly* understand, I think it's time that I told you the story of the Harvest."

"No need, Mom. Nana used to tell it to me as a bedtime story."

"You'll find this version a little different," August said. He ducked his eyes and let Bianca take over.

"I was just a teenager. We went camping, my parents and I. It wasn't something we did often, even though my Dad loved the outdoors.

"That summer, for who knows what reason, Dad realized that I was getting older and that soon I'd be gone…off to college. So, desperate to create some memories, he and Mother planned the camping trip.

"I didn't want to go. I had big plans for the summer. Pulling me away from my friends and into the deep woods was not part of them. I acted like a spoiled child."

Bianca bit her lip and looked at her nervous hands.

"It's alright," August urged.

Her eyes shone as she continued, "On that night, we had a huge argument. I stormed from the RV. I cursed them under my breath as I pitched a pup tent and climbed inside.

"It was very late. I kept dozing off as I was reading. The air went cold, and before I knew it, my tent was filled with them. The shadows. Like a thick fog, they rolled into the tent and over me. I kicked. I fought, but my hands went right through them. I tried to scream, but they covered my mouth.

"I woke up beside a great bonfire. I didn't see the fire, though. Not at first. As I rolled on my side, familiar brown eyes stared back at me, unblinking.

"I asked, 'Where are we?' but Mother didn't answer. She couldn't. She was already gone.

"I screamed so hard, I thought I had ripped my vocal chords. And it drew unwanted attention.

"Grief completely overwhelmed me. The tears blurred everything. I couldn't see straight. I could just feel the pressure of him on me."

August squeezed her hand tighter. Bianca spared him a glance before continuing.

"Bov Gammen held my wrists and, for a moment, I thought that he was there to rescue me. I thought he was going to pull me up from the ground. Then he bit. His fangs sank into the vein at my wrist.

"I pleaded. I asked him to stop, but my voice was gone. Still, he lifted his head and said something to me. Something about being special. Something about being delicious. Something about his need to savor…No, 'savor' wasn't the word he used. Control. He wanted to control my blood, keep it all for himself, so 'not a drop was squandered on peasants'.

"He released my wrist, and stood over me. He kicked my mother's body so that she was positioned flat on her back before he picked her up and carried her over his shoulder like a sack of potatoes.

"My head swam, but I managed to sit up and wipe my eyes clear. Bodies were stacked all around. The shadows were continuing to arrive with new humans in tow. They kept coming.

"I remember seeing a girl my age in a short, blue dress. It was one that I had tried on just weeks before when I thought that I would be out partying with my friends. Her eyes were blank. Her chest didn't move.

"Seeing this girl, dressed this way, I came to realize that the shadows weren't just taking people from the forest. They were hunting in the towns too. In some cases, dragging their victims for miles.

"I didn't know it then, but human blood is a delicacy to mogdocs. Bov was gaining favor by stockpiling humans, collecting enough so that the entire Empire could eat like kings for a year."

"But you fought back," Keira said as though it was a matter of fact.

Bianca nodded. Keira could tell that she was straining to hold back tears.

"Bov could not stay away. He found my blood too compelling. Eventually, he came back to me. Only this time, I was ready. I think, " she paused, "I think he was shocked that I was fighting back. His shock, his hesitation, helped me escape more than anything I could have done. Once I was out of his reach, I tumbled down the thick brush of the hillside, just like in the story."

"The *Girl Who Got Away,*" Keira breathed.

"The *Girl Who Got Away,*" Bianca repeated. Their brown eyes locked, unmoving until Bianca's eyes flicked to August as if she were trying to decide if she should speak the thought that she was thinking.

"Mom, what is it?" Keira asked.

"I don't want you anywhere near the Harvest."

"Wait! What?"

"Keira, listen to me," Bianca said, her voice steadier than it had been before. "If Broo is trying to pull off the Harvest, she is doing it because she has lost favor with her subjects. I can't think of a better way to prove herself than to bring back the blood of the *Girl Who Got Away* or better yet, her daughter, the guardian child of sun and moon."

"But, Mom, if this is happening, I've got to stop it. There is no one else."

"If this is happening, it will take more than one person to stop it. You don't even know what you're up against. There are *hordes* of shadows. They cannot be reasoned with."

"I don't care," Keira shook her head with an intensity normally reserved for frilly dresses.

"You don't care? Really?" Bianca asked, though it was clearly not a real question. "You're talking about a suicide mission. I'm the only one to ever escape the Harvest, and I'm only here because of dumb luck. I barely got out with my life. I was done, dying at the bottom of the ravine when they found me the next morning."

"I'm not you."

"No, you're not. You are a child. My child, and that is precisely why you cannot get involved in this."

"It's not up to you."

"August?" Bianca's eyes flew to her husband for help.

"Dad?" Keira's eyes were on him too.

Unfortunately for them, he wasn't going to choose a side, at least not publicly. August pushed his hands in his pockets. His lips touched Bianca's cheek and kissed it softly.

"I'll join you in a little while," he whispered.

Keira's mother took her exit, giving them both warning glares as she disappeared from the doorway.

August watched his soul mate leave. When the master bedroom door slammed, the corner of his mouth turned up. "And you thought you got your stubbornness from me."

"Dad, I…" Keira started to explain, but he cut her off.

"Tell me about the mogdoc prince, Gammen's son."

Keira's eyes turned to the window. Her father's question warranted another sip of sweet orange goodness.

"I don't know. Arden doesn't trust him; neither does Colby."

"Nicola seems to think that there might be something to his theory," he said, his forehead crinkled in the middle. "I won't lie to you. I wasn't pleased to hear it. However, she said that she had never seen you as happy as when the two of you courted. That love is perhaps the greatest human gift there is."

"Courted? Seriously?" she smiled despite herself. "Hold it! You've been talking to Nana?"

August ignored the question and instead returned

with his own, "He's living at the Citadel?"

She nodded. "He comes and goes. He doesn't seem to have any royal obligations. They don't trust him either."

"That's usually a trait that the mogdocs look for in a leader."

"I guess they don't think he's worthy."

"And his sister?"

"She trusts him…well that, or she thinks it's better to keep him close. I don't think she would ever hurt him. She's had her chance and didn't take it, but with her, who knows?"

"Hmmm," he leaned back. "You realize, I asked you to tell me about him and you've told me what everyone else thinks of him."

She shrugged. It was easier to give him everyone else's opinions. He should have known that before he asked. She leaned forward and put a hand on the window sash.

"Keira?"

"Hmmm," she said, lost in the night outside.

"Do you think he is right? Do you think that you and the prince are destined to be together?"

"No. Maybe. I don't know," Keira said, shaking his words from her head. "I'm gonna go outside and check something out. Wanna come?"

He hesitated.

"Or we can continue this really awkward talk. Or you could go tell Mom that I'm stopping the Harvest, and there's nothing she can do about it."

"Let's go," he said.

August pivoted and worked the latch on the wooden cabinet behind him. Its glass inset doors reflected Keira's face back. The girl she saw in that reflection was different. She basically looked like Keira–dark hair and eyes, naturally pink cheeks, sun-kissed skin–but she was thinner and her eyes were tired.

August carefully selected a crossbow for himself. He tossed Keira a staff, and as he secured the crossbow sling across his chest, he heard his daughter say, “A stick? Really?”

August turned to see her twirling it like a drum major’s baton.

“Let’s see what you can do with it. You still have your dagger on you if we find ourselves in a sticky wicket, correct?”

She nodded, all the while fighting the urge to tease him about his word choice.

That nod was good enough for him. They were off. Keira flipped the back porch light off before opening the door. She pointed him toward the soybean field that separated their house from Colby and Jamie’s homes.

Heavy with pods, the waist-high soybean plants bobbed in the night air. Keira walked the rows carefully, her father right behind.

“No flashlights,” had been Keira’s instruction. Only the full moon lit their path. Keira took the lead with her father following closely behind.

“I think,” she said. “I think I saw him out here. He’s been watching me for a very long time.”

It was easier to admit knowing that August could not see her face.

“What do you mean by watching you?”

“Just looking out for me. I think he kinda feels responsible for me or something,” Keira brushed it off.

She may have thought nothing of it, but her dismissal did nothing to ease August's concern.

"Sweetheart, do you think that this mogdoc boy could really be in love with you?"

There it was. Keira stopped dead in her tracks. Her fingers went to her sides and fidgeted with the hem of her shirt. "Dad…I…"

"At some point, it will matter." He put a hand on her arm. "I will not make your choices for you, but know this. Mogdocs don't love."

"Yeah, I've heard that before," she said with a roll of her eyes.

As if on cue, the full moon reached down and dusted everything with a brilliant luminosity. The two, father and daughter, stood alone in the field.

As he looked at her, the concern written all over his face, she began to feel guilty about blowing off his words. She started to say something, but he was first.

"You've heard it before, but has anyone ever actually explained why? For mogdocs, love finds them just as it does any other creature in nature. However, their love is contaminated by jealousy and greed. Their very nature turns love into obsession. Keira, mogdocs don't love, because they don't know how."

August's words hung on the air as the two continued down the path through the field in silence. Keira stopped when they stepped from the rows. August came up beside her.

"There," she said.

August followed her hand as it raised into the air. A figure sat on the roof of Colby's house.

"Is it your friend?" August asked, trying to fix his eyes on the dark figure.

"It's Brun."

"What is he doing?"

"Watching. Guarding maybe. From that vantage point, he can see anything that approaches Drew's window. You know, Brun said that he had taken Drew because there were others after him. He was trying to protect my charge," she explained.

"If it isn't safe, then why did he bring Drew back?"

Keira had wondered that herself. It was all too easy. Why go through all the trouble of kidnapping Drew, only to give him back so quickly. Was Drew back because Brun truly thought that he had thwarted the Sect's or the Unionists' attempts? Or…she let her mind wander, was Drew back because Brun was afraid of what she was willing to sacrifice to rescue him?

Keira shook the questions from her head before continuing.

"I didn't tell Colby, but Brun's been doing this all summer. I spotted him the second night we stayed in the tent. I'm not sure what to make of it. He just sits and watches." Her nervous hand moved from pointing to the figure on the roof of Colby's two-story farmhouse to the darkened window of little Drew's bedroom in the modular house next door.

"Did you confront him?"

"I've talked to him, but no, not about this. I'm not sure I'd get the entire truth. Mogdocs lie, remember?"

August shook his head. "I was so wrapped up in what was going on, on the other side of the barrier. I had no idea."

"Now you do," she smiled. "And I could really use your help."

Concealed at the edge of the field, the two crouched and waited. As the night wore on, August ordered Keira to bed with the promise that he would stay and watch over her charge. She didn't attempt dissent. It was no use. After all, it was a school night.

* * *

Waking up in her real bed felt foreign. Keira had spent so many nights in the tent that she came to forget the comfort that comes with a mattress and box springs. The morning sun peeked in the window, and tried to drive her out of bed. She blocked it with a pillow and rolled over. Then it was her alarm clock's turn. She slapped the snooze button only a couple of times before finally succumbing to its call.

Keira had just pulled on her favorite cowboy boots when Colby pulled in the driveway. She and Arden had planned on walking. Colby's presence was a surprise.

Colby knocked on the door like a perfect gentleman, dressed in new dark jeans and a light blue t-shirt that made his sapphire eyes look even brighter and deeper somehow.

Keira opened the door, already in defense mode. He wouldn't drive them to school every day. She made that clear from the start. He would have, but she insisted on her independence. It wasn't a surprise. He knew she would.

However, being that it was the first day of senior year and that she did not have her own car, she took him up on his offer with the understanding that it wasn't permanent.

Colby sniggered at her explanation. Of course, that's what senior year was all about…the lack of permanence.

"Shotgun!"

Arden was quick. She would give him that. Keira pursed her lips and gave him a look that could kill as he took the front passenger seat for his own. She let him get away with it, but made sure it was as uncomfortable as possible for him when she shoved the seat forward to take her place in the back.

Keira listened to Colby and Arden the whole way and barely said a word. Too soon the school was in sight. Keira had forgotten all about the special parking spaces for seniors. Though she didn't say so, she was absolutely impressed when Colby pulled into his own freshly bordered, assigned space next to the gym.

The school smelled new. New clothes on the students. New paint in the hallways. New books in the classrooms. Keira followed the new smells to homeroom, leaving Colby and Arden behind.

"She's distracted," Arden worried.

"She's okay," Colby said aloud.

"She hasn't been okay for a while and you know it."

He did. Above it all, he was her best friend. How could he not know? He watched her struggle under the stop and wait orders from the guardian elders. He stood by as she wrestled with her fear for Drew's future. Yet, those were not the things that concerned Colby most. One thing, one person, distracted Keira more than anything.

"So what do we do about it?" Colby asked.

"Nothing we can do. It's all about her."

"Isn't it always?"

"Yeah," Arden chuckled. "Seems that way. Has she told you about the Council?"

"She mentioned that a couple of them are starting to side with the Unionists. Is it true? Do they think that Keira and Brun's baby will be the gift from the prophecy?"

Arden scrunched up his nose. It was enough to tell Colby that it was true.

"How bad is it?" Colby asked.

"Honestly?" Arden shrugged. "I think it's the least of our worries."

"She said something like that too; something about Broo getting overthrown by the Sect of Low."

"My worry *is* Broo and what she's willing to do to prove herself. There's a very old tradition…wait…where would Keira get the idea that the Sect was planning a coup?"

"Where do you think?" Colby answered. And even before the words passed his lips, he knew he had said too much. Arden's face went blank with fury as Colby realized he was reading out of a book in which Arden hadn't made it past the dedication. No, they weren't on the same page at all. Arden didn't know she'd been talking to Brun.

Colby darted into the classroom, only to find Arden following him in; not that he actually turned around to see him. He didn't have to. He could hear Arden breathe behind him, fast and heavy like he had been sucker punched in the stomach.

As it turned out, they had both been assigned to the same homeroom, Room 101A, Mrs. Bethany. Colby made his way toward the front, as he always did. Arden kept his eyes locked on him, but chose to sit in the back.

Chapter 10: Bird's Eye View

Colby worried the whole morning, and rightly so. Keira was going to kill him. The best friend code lay broken at his feet. He had inadvertently yet effectively tattled to the babysitter.

He tried to make himself feel better about it, tapping into the pain he felt in watching Keira go back to Brun again and again. Maybe, just maybe, she would listen to Arden. Arden, her mentor, could stop her from seeing Brun.

Arden fumed the whole morning. He nearly knocked Colby over when he brushed by him between classes. The longer he thought about Keira speaking to the mogdoc prince, the angrier he became. Keira was his apprentice, and she had learned nothing.

He told her. He told her not to trust him. Still, she ran straight to Brun. Again. Bile rose in his throat as he thought about her in Gammen's arms, his smug face sniffing her raven hair as he whispered evil in her ear.

Arden jerked up with a start in fourth period. He was on his feet in front of the whole class before he realized it.

"I uh," he breathed heavily, sick from his imagination. Random muffled laughs sounded around him. "I need a bit of fresh air, sir, I feel I'm not…may I…"

Sure that Arden was about to revisit his breakfast, Mr. Norwood gave a quick nod of permission and waved him toward the door.

The hallway was empty. Arden's footsteps were the only sound, slow at first, then picking up speed. He blew past the last classrooms and pushed the bar to open the steel door at the hall's end.

Inside one of those classrooms, Keira idly chewed on her pencil. She didn't know what page they were on, but she knew how many birds had landed on the tree outside the window. Ann sat at the desk beside her. They had barely talked all period. It was their only class together, but Ann was furiously scribbling away.

Notes probably, Keira thought.

The teacher was going on and on about something. It must have been important. Every few words, he would stop so that the note takers could catch up.

A wing of blue caught Keira's eye. That was number eight in the tree. The bird was a beautiful blue, very near the shade of the lights in the sky over the Atlantean beach where Brun had tried to kiss her.

And there it was. She was thinking about him

again. Her muscles tightened and before she knew it, she had broken her pencil in half. Ann turned to her with wide eyes. In them was a plea to put the pieces away and pretend like it never happened.

Keira peered at the halves, wanting so badly to groan or scream.

"What's wrong?" Ann whispered.

Keira mouthed "nothing" and shoved the pieces of the broken pencil into her backpack. To prove that everything was alright, she took a cleansing breath and turned back to her beautiful blue bird.

It was even more wondrous now with wings spread wide in full flight; though it no longer had her attention. No, now her eyes were on the two boys coming to blows at the base of the tree.

Her hand shot up.

In less than a minute, Keira slipped out the door with a restroom pass in hand. She hit the hall in dead run.

"Tell me! What are you doing here?" Arden yelled. One hand gripped Brun's shirt, the other was fisted and pulled back to strike again.

Brun laughed at him, even as blood started to stream down his forehead. "Go back to class, rat, before you get suspended, or heaven forbid, expelled."

Arden gritted his teeth and threw the power of his whole body forward. Just as he was about to connect, Keira stepped in and pushed him back. He stumbled a few steps before recovering his balance. He went very still as Keira used the edge of her sleeve to wipe the blood from Brun's face.

"Keira! Get away from him! He was stalking you," Arden sneered, his voice low and dark, almost a growl.

Brun looked into her eyes, eyes that reminded him of steaming hot cocoa, as she asked, "Is that true?"

"These are dangerous times," Brun replied without even a hint of guilt or remorse.

"Well then," she said. "It makes sense that he would keep tabs on me with everything that's going on. Arden, that's no reason to pummel him in front of the whole school. Is there anything else? Can we go back inside now, boys?"

Brun took that as his signal to leave. He put his fist to his chest and gave a slight bow before turning and using his inhuman speed to disappear into the trees that bordered the back of the school property.

"Have you gone insane? What are you doing with him? He's a mogdoc. He can't be trusted."

"I'm not *with* him, Arden. Besides, he's more human than me," she finally uttered, collapsing onto the grass in a cross-legged heap in preparation for Arden's oncoming lecture.

Arden sighed. "And you are both more human than me. Why are you being such a fool? Blood doesn't matter. It's the heart itself that matters."

"Then quit throwing it in my face that he's a mogdoc!" she rounded on him. "I know what's in his heart, Arden. He saved my life. He's guarding Drew. He's trying to figure this all out. All for me."

"That's what he wants you to think."

"Don't give me that. He was raised as a mogdoc. That's the only reason why he comes off so obsessive. Dad says he doesn't know how to love."

Arden towered above her, his soul heavy. Keira tilted her head up to him, but he wouldn't look at her. An overwhelming feeling of dread settled over her. He was going to extend her training schedule. He was going to bar her from crossing the barrier. She ran through the list of possible punishments. Whatever he selected, it didn't matter. This now, this silence, was worse than anything he could dream up.

He just breathed. He didn't say a word. He wouldn't look at her. The moments wore on and she wondered what he was waiting for.

"I can't watch this happen," he finally said to her surprise. "The Council. Now you. You have made a grave mistake in letting him get too close to you."

"Arden, wait…"

She unfolded her legs and rocked onto her feet, but it was too late. Her mentor was gone.

* * *

"Please stop and think about this, Arden," Bianca pleaded. "My daughter needs all the help she can get. For heaven's sake, it's the Harvest."

"I *have* thought about this," he said and it was the truth. His day had been plagued by the memory of Keira gently wiping the blood from the wounds that he had inflicted on Brun's perfect face. Well, it wasn't so perfect anymore.

Arden refused to look Bianca's way. Instead, he placed another book into the cardboard box on his desk. Packing should have been a simple task. However, in addition to the massive collection of books he brought with him, he had accumulated dozens more with his research on the prophecy over the last year.

"August, will you talk some sense into him?"

Keira's father, August Ryan, slouched in the

doorway and watched. With hands neatly tucked into the pockets of his khakis, he looked completely comfortable. “If the boy wants to go…”

Arden’s lips curled, and he placed another book in the box. If anyone could do anything about this situation, it was August Ryan, he thought. All he had to do was forbid Keira from contact with the mogdoc prince. He couldn’t understand why August allowed it in the first place. By his own inaction, August was choosing this for his daughter. The thought of that disgusted Arden even more.

“…of course,” August continued with a hand now reaching to rub the dark stubble on his chin. “If he leaves now, he gives up his own place in history.”

Arden stopped. He stabled himself with both hands on the box. His eyes seemed as fire though his voice remained steady. “You mean my place as mentor behind the greatest guardian to ever live. What good is it? She doesn’t listen to me. It’s a sham.”

“No, Arden,” Bianca reached for him.

Anger clenched his jaw. “I’ve made my decision.” He placed another book in the box.

“Come on, sweet, leave him be,” August said, sweeping his wife out of the room. Their hushed argument continued down the hallway.

Arden picked up the mailing tape dispenser that August left for him. It was a handy tool with a cutter on the end. He slammed it down on top of the box, and pulled so that the tape screeched out. He finished with a slight flick of his wrist.

Arden tossed the box aside and blew out a breath of relief. His body collapsed onto the edge of the bed. Hands pulled their way over his tired face.

Books in piles surrounded him. He grabbed the

one on top of the nearest stack, giving it a quick glance as he moved to toss it into the next box. However, he stopped before it left his hand.

It gave him reason to pause. He flipped through the pages of the book he remembered so fondly. He had read it so many times as a child; though it was never considered to be appropriate children's reading.

His fingers smoothed over the red leather cover; then over the letters embossed on its spine, *The Hayes Prophecies*. Its gilded pages were slightly faded. It wasn't the real thing, just a reproduction. The original sat on a shelf in Keira's training room in Elsted. Still, it held very real memories for him. He flipped through the pages and let their scent take him back to his favorite chair in the magic-induced sunlight of Nedda's study where he dreamed of being the hero, the child of sun and moon destined to thwart the monsters and save the world.

He was part of it now, part of the prophecy. Giving that up should hurt. It didn't. The pain, he realized, was in staying.

With great care, he lowered the book in a new box, but another was already there.

"What's this?" he asked aloud though no one was there to answer.

The worn, brown leather cover was stiff like wood. It was much smaller than the other books of its age. Maybe that's why he had overlooked it before. It must have been stuffed among the volumes that he took with him when he left Nedda's library for the last time. His fingers ran over the symbol of a tall feather stamped on the front.

"Ahem." August cleared his throat as he leaned in the doorway. "For what it's worth, I'm not going to ask what happened. I'm just going to ask you to move beyond it. The Elders aren't going to help her."

"Did Mrs. Ryan make you come back?"

"Maybe," he shrugged. "But she's right. It's just us and what little luck we have left."

"Maybe there's more than a little," Arden smiled, tossing the book to August. "I've just found a reason to stay."

August flipped the book over. "This can't be? The feather of Ma'at?"

"The Egyptian goddess of balance and order," Arden added with more than a dash of nerd-like zeal. "Oh, I should have known. That Nedda...wonderful, brilliant Nedda. Stolen the lost. I did! I stole it. She knew, knew it all along. I could kiss her. I could kiss *you!"*

"You don't mean? This little book? Are you sure?"

"August, she was trying to tell me that I had taken the answer from her very library. This is it; what you've been looking for all that time in Elsted. It was here the whole time. I'm sure of it. This is the *Book of the Lost."*

"Arden, do you know what this means?"

Arden looked to August. His lips rose in the corners. His brow lifted ever higher.

"Hope."

Chapter 11: Sweet Kick in the Dairy Dog

Keira swung by the newspaper office after her last class. Sure enough, Ann was there. One pencil tucked behind her ear, she wrote with another breaking only to occasionally scroll through the computer screen.

Keira plopped into the chair by her desk. Her desk. Ann had her own desk. Keira was surprised at how natural her friend looked behind it.

Being the new senior editor of the school newspaper certainly had its advantages. Keira sifted through the invites and free tickets filling the wire bin that Ann used as a mailbox. It was as if her cocoon burst open and out sprang Miss Social Butterfly.

As Keira had her eyes down, Ann peeked up from her work.

"Rumor mill says Arden cut his last classes," the

red-head said. She moved to the front of the desk and sat on its edge. The pencil still teetered over her ear. "Care to comment."

"Off the record," Keira curved her lips upward. "Guys are all drama. I'll probably be grounded tomorrow, so I was hoping for a little girl time tonight."

"Come on, then." Ann put the pencil down, gave her hair a shake, and scooped up Keira by the arm.

"No, you have work to do."

"Eh," Ann waved it away. "I'll make the freshman do it tomorrow. Deadline's not 'til Thursday."

"It's true. It's good to be the boss," Keira smiled.

The girls walked and talked until they wound up at Dairy Dog, a seasonal hotdog/ice cream stand a few blocks from the high school. It hadn't been their intention, the music lured them in.

Sweet Kick, a local garage band that was a favorite of Keira and her friends, was set up in the gazebo. The bass had just started warming up.

The picnic tables surrounding the hotdog stand were full. Keira made her way to the back while Ann ordered a couple of cherry limeades.

"You and Jump going to Fall Ball?" Keira asked as soon as Ann returned.

Ann took a long draw from her straw and nodded. Keira could practically see her mind at work.

"Why don't we double? I'm sure Jump's got a teammate that could..."

"No, thanks," Keira threw a hand up. "I'd rather not spend the night listening to old football stories. Besides, I'm kind of surprised that you're going."

"Why is that?"

"You know," Keira shrugged. "The last dance we went to put you in the hospital."

"I'm not letting Broo keep me from the last Fall Ball. We're seniors. This is the time to make memories that will last our entire lives. I'm not spending the year in hiding. No regrets."

"No regrets," Keira repeated her friend's words, and the two bumped their cups before taking another sip as if it were a toast.

"I can't imagine that you have regrets."

The voice came out of thin air and too close for comfort. Keira nearly spit out her drink as she whirled around to find the speaker.

As she turned, she was met by an eagle inked in black, half hidden under a tight t-shirt sleeve. The boy it belonged to had his back to her, having somehow wedged himself between the two friends. A pair of drumsticks stuck out of his back pockets where his thumbs were hooked loosely. He was talking to Ann.

Keira edged around him to get a good look. The boy was gorgeous and the cocky smile plastered on his face told Keira that he knew it. He was not skinny, but lean, and very tall, a basketball coach's dream. Golden blond hair fell in his dark eyes that sparkled a little by the lights that had come on due to approaching twilight. He pushed those golden strands back with long, nimble fingers which then fell to his hips.

"Come to hear me play?" the boy asked Ann.

"What time do you start?"

"In just a few. Where's Johnny?"

"Umm, it's Jumper," Ann looked to the ground. "Just us, it's girls' night. Eric, this is my friend Keira, Keira Ryan."

"Hey, Keira," he said.

Keira tipped her head up. Not that Eric would notice. He didn't bother so much as a glance her way.

"How's that article going?"

"Pretty good. I finally got hold of the superintendent. Looks like he's going to give me a quote."

"Sweet," Eric replied, his smile even wider than before. "So, I gotta go. Enjoy the show and I'll catch you later."

Keira watched the boy walk away, and then turned to her friend.

"Who was that?"

"That, my friend, is Eric Jansen. I met him when I interviewed the band last week."

Eric Jansen was Sweet Kick's new drummer. Last year, the band's original drummer split for college. They had gone through a few different guys since then. The new guy, Keira thought, seemed promising. Even if he couldn't play, he would certainly attract plenty of new female fans.

"You must have made an impression on him."

"What do you mean?" Ann asked indifferently as she adjusted her straw over the ice in her cup.

"You know what I mean."

"Does anybody?"

"Seriously?"

"What are you talking about?"

"Ann," Keira said pointedly. "That guy was totally into you."

"Whatever. He was just being nice. Besides, he knows I'm with Jumper."

"Yeah, sounds like he thinks *Johnny* is stiff competition," Keira laughed.

"He's trouble," Ann said. "Forget about Eric. He

collects girlfriends like Pez dispensers."

Keira grinned, "Poor boy needs somewhere to keep all that eye candy."

Ann rolled her eyes and chucked her empty cup into the trash. "Hey, there's Mikey."

She took Keira's arm and pulled her to the werewolf girl. Mikey balanced atop a railing near the side of the gazebo.

As she always did, Keira took note of her dress. It didn't disappoint. She was dripping with her usual cool.

On that night she wore a skin-tight, vintage Grateful Dead t-shirt under a fitted black leather jacket. Dark jeans sat notoriously low on her hips with studded black cowboy boots beneath.

Her hair had been flattened to lay perfectly straight. It seemed longer than Keira recalled, nearly reaching the middle of the girl's back. Then Keira realized that she had just never before seen Mikey's hair without curl, wave, or some weird contortion.

Keira welcomed the distraction. Ann wouldn't bring up Arden's absence again in Mikey's presence. They were still learning how to trust Mikey.

By the time the girls reached Mikey, the band had launched into an original rock party anthem; something that they called "Outside In" which featured their new drummer.

Ann tried to hop on top of the railing, her short legs struggling a bit, as Keira leaned nonchalantly against it. Mikey acknowledged the girls with a lift of her chin. An earbud dangled at her chest, the other firmly placed in her ear.

"Listenin' to a little music while you listen to a little music?" Keira smirked.

"What?" Mikey yelled over the band.

Keira pointed to the girl's ear, as the band finished the song.

"Oh yeah, this," she raised her phone so that Keira could see it. "I'm sampling them. Going to do a mash-up later."

"And they're okay with that?" Ann asked.

Mikey tilted her head, "I used to date the drummer. They're cool with it."

Ann shot Keira that *I told you so* look.

"So, what brings the two of you out on a school night?" Mikey asked in a way that made them unsure if she truly did want to know or if she was just making fun of them. Maybe both.

"Just hanging out," Keira tried to play off coolly.

"Yeah, I see," her eyes searched them. "And where's your puppy dog crew?"

"It's girls' night," Ann answered, raising her voice as the band slipped into its next song.

Keira couldn't help but wonder why Ann kept calling it that. Like it was a real thing. Like it was something planned. Still, the answer satisfied Mikey all the same. She went back to fiddling with her phone and earbuds.

Ann pushed next to Keira.

"I was serious before about getting you a date for the Ball," Ann said. "You know it doesn't have to be someone from the team."

"I'm not going."

"You're not?" Ann seemed put off by Keira's response. "Didn't you hear my whole impassioned speech about this being senior year and no regrets?"

"Well, here's the deal," Keira lowered her shoulders. "I thought it would be a good idea to stand guard outside. If Broo tries to make another appearance, I want to be ready. So I'll be at the dance, just not inside."

"That's actually kind of astute."

"What are you two cluckin' about?" Mikey burst in.

Ann answered immediately, not at all offended by Mikey's hen reference, "Fall Ball. Are you going?"

"Yeah, that blond guy asked me."

Keira's eyes narrowed. "Blond guy?"

She was sure Mikey had said she "used to" date the drummer. Past tense.

Mikey yanked the earbud from her ear and looked Keira directly in the eyes. The music was too loud. Keira watched Mikey's burgundy-stained lips as they moved slowly like in a dream…or a nightmare.

"You know him actually," the werewolf girl said, a wicked smile began to grow.

"Teacher's Pet."

Chapter 12: The Final Ball

Keira didn't slap the werewolf, but she wanted to. Boy, did she want to. Her thoughts drifted back to that night as she sat on the roof of the school.

The sky was dark and full of stars. The decorated, wavy blade of her father's kris gleamed against her black clothing as it lay in her lap.

Couples had been arriving for the last hour. At first, they came in large droves, but as the night wore on, the crowds dwindled.

Keira sat up a little straighter when Colby's car pulled into the lot. She watched him duck out of the car and walk around to the passenger's side. He opened the door for his date.

"Who does that anymore?" Keira said to no one as she grabbed up her binoculars.

Mikey took his hand and stepped from the car.

He was shaking. His heartbeat overwhelmed her werewolf hearing.

As soon as she was on her feet, Mikey let go to smooth down her dress. It was strapless, long, and form-fitting; a simple dress with black beading and an exaggerated slit which revealed her muscled, right leg.

Colby stood nervously beside her. His hands were pushed into the pockets of his black tuxedo. When she was done primping, they started to walk toward the gym.

Keira started when Mikey stopped. The werewolf girl whispered something in Colby's ear and then kissed him. Right there in the middle of the parking lot.

It wasn't a quick peck on the lips either. His hands gripped Mikey's shoulders, but her hands, they were all over him. She broke off with a gasp. Keira threw her binoculars down.

Jumper's Jeep screeched into the parking lot. Colby and Mikey waited as the red-headed couple approached. The four talked as they walked, but she couldn't hear their words from her station atop the school.

Near the entrance, Ann stopped and pointed Keira out to the rest of them. She gave a small wave.

Even from that distance, she could see Colby's eyes flash wide as he realized that Keira had been there the whole time. He grabbed Mikey's hand and rushed inside.

Keira exhaled deeply.

Good, she thought.

Something in her was glad that he'd been embarrassed. However, her satisfaction didn't last long. Guilt crept in. He wasn't her boyfriend, after all.

It wasn't up to her who he did and did not date. This was good for him, she told herself. He was moving on. Who was she to say that he shouldn't be with Mikey? He wasn't hers.

As if her thoughts had summoned him, she caught sight of Brun on the other side of the roof. He was carefully making his way in her direction.

She noticed that he was dressed in dark jeans and a jacket. He was dressed for warmth and stealth, just like she was.

"Thought you could use a warm-up," he smiled, producing a Thermos from behind his back.

"Sure. How did you know I was here?"

"Seriously?"

She laughed despite herself.

"It's was the least I could do," he said as he poured her a cup of the warm brew. "Since you stitched me up."

"Thanks," she said. She took the cup in her hand and let the steam warm her face.

"Are you healing?"

He nodded and lifted his shirt to expose his left side. "Good as new."

Keira made sure that her eyes didn't linger. She looked quickly and took a sip from the cup.

And immediately choked. She had assumed it was coffee or cocoa, but it wasn't. This drink had a strange taste, full of spices and honey and something else.

"Is this going to get me drunk?" she asked, giving him a sideways glance.

"Maybe a little," he smiled slyly. "Drink up."

Keira laughed and put the cup down. The drink was already starting to warm her insides. It felt good.

She almost wished that she could take in more of it, but she knew it was a bad idea. Her mind needed to stay sharp.

Brun gulped the rest of his cup. He balanced the empty cup and Thermos on top of an air vent, before sitting down beside her.

"I don't think you're going to see much action tonight. Broo went to bed about an hour ago."

"Good to know," Keira said. She directed her eyes back to the parking lot.

"There's still time."

"For what?"

"Well, if you wanted to go to the dance."

"I'm fine up here."

"I could have a dress here in seconds, and if you don't have a date…"

"What? You're offering?"

"Why not?" he chuckled to himself. "I would love to look back on this night and remember us dancing."

"Yeah, well," she said with a roll of her eyes. It was funny how the drink had affected him so quickly. She didn't even feel a buzz.

"I don't' think that's a good idea." She turned to him. "Like I said, I'm fine up here. Good night, Brun."

"Good night, Keira," he said, not bothering to hide his disappointment.

She couldn't stand it. She had to look away.

Beside her, he leaned down and whispered, "I'll leave the Thermos in case you want some more later."

"Wait, Brun…" she looked up, but he was already gone.

Her eyes continued to search for him. If it weren't for that, she may not have noticed the blue flickers, like fireflies, dancing among the trees bordering the parking lot.

She grabbed up her binoculars to take a better look. Just as she had suspected, they weren't fireflies. They were magical little creatures called will 'o wisps. The last time she had seen one was at Nana's birthday party.

The wisps darted among the trees. Then, suddenly, a mogdoc stepped from them. First one, then another, and another until there were five in all. Five.

"The Sect of Low," she breathed.

Keira dropped the binoculars, picked up the sword from her lap, and scrambled to her feet. She jogged the length of the roof to its edge and took a running leap.

When she looked up, the mogdocs had disappeared into the trees. She stepped lightly to follow them.

Keira avoided the sticks and leaves as best she could to remain undetected once she entered the tree line. The mogdocs' voices were clear. They had stopped, and were not far from her. They seemed to be talking, not to each other, but to someone else.

"The fifth has been completed. We are pleased," she heard one of the creatures rasp.

The voice came from beyond the underbrush ahead of her. She ducked under its cover and listened.

"Then you will stand down?"

This time it was not a mogdoc's screeching words. Those words were spoken by a woman. A brave woman. There was no sign of intimidation in her voice as she spoke to the most lethal creatures alive. Keira flexed her hand, bringing the kris close to her side.

"For now," the mogdoc sneered back. "But take heed, for if he does not act on this…" it paused for a moment to search for the right word, "…opportunity, then our hand will be forced."

The woman took in his words. Keira moved to try to get a look at her. It was useless. Her dark shape hovered just behind a tree.

"Do not try to threaten me, Valik," the woman's voice rose. "You have seen it with your own eyes. You know what is to come."

"Perhaps."

"Perhaps is a word for the undecided."

An acorn tumbled onto Keira's shoulder. She brushed it away without thinking. The nut landed just feet away, rustling as it settled into the dry leaves.

The Sect raised their weapons. The woman stopped talking. Valik jerked his head toward the sound. His eyes urgently ordered one of the other mogdocs to the spot.

Keira held her breath. Her body stilled.

The mogdoc took his sword and stabbed at the underbrush. He ambled to the side and turned over a log. A squirrel popped out of the end and darted off.

The mogdoc's green eyes lit with delight. With inhuman speed, it pounced on the woodland creature, snapped its neck and dangled its lifeless body from its belt. The mogdoc patted his kill proudly as if thinking about the fine snack it would make later as he rejoined the circle.

Keira stifled the urge to throw up. She turned her attention back to the woman.

Though Keira couldn't see the woman's face, she suspected that she found it to be incorrigible. Valik, however, gave Squirrel Slayer an approving nod.

"Valik!" the woman demanded his attention. "Where do you stand?"

The sound of her reprimand struck something in Keira, something familiar. Yet she couldn't put her finger on it.

Valik replied, "Our loyalty, as always, is to the Empire, but where, dear woman, will your loyalties lie when all has come to pass?"

The woman sighed, but Keira didn't hear her answer.

Valik smiled a smile so vile that it made Keira's skin crawl. He said, "The five will bond us all. So it is done."

"So it is done," the woman repeated after him.

That voice. A woman's voice, soft yet commanding and wise…familiar.

"Nana!"

Keira burst from the brush, pushing the kris in the air before her.

* * *

"But you *knew* she was watching," Colby's hands rose in wide gestures over his head. "You knew!"

"What's your issue? You wanted to make her jealous. You were doing a lousy job. I helped. End of story," Mikey shrugged. "You're welcome."

"I didn't want to…ahhh…" Colby put a hand on his forehead. "This isn't happening. Jump, this was a terrible idea. Why did I listen to you?"

"Yeah, I'd think you would know better," Jumper smirked.

Ann stepped in. "Listen, it's not the end of the

world."

Colby looked down to her, his eyes were big and sad, but he knew that she was right.

"Could anyone see her face? How did she look?"

Mikey, Jumper, and Ann were suddenly distracted by the decorations in the gym.

"How did she look?" he repeated.

* * *

"You have betrayed us," the mogdocs hissed.

The five brandished their weapons. She had been right. They were the Sect of Low, Gammen's version of the knights of the round table, selected of the empire's most skilled warriors. Keira inhaled and steadied herself.

The two closest Keira charged her. Her kris caught under the sword of the first one and lifted it over the mogdoc's head.

Her sword still in the air, she kicked at the other. It fell on its back. She brought her sword down and swung it again at the first mogdoc, this time disarming it.

Both charged her together, with one wide swoop, she took them both out. The other three creatures screeched and started toward her.

"Enough!" Nana's voice boomed. "Her presence changes nothing."

The mogdocs froze.

Nana looked at them as she picked her way across the grass. She stood in front of Keira. Her hair as white and her cheeks as rosy as they had ever been. Her five tails rose behind her and whisked from side to side.

"What's going on?" Keira whispered.

Nana took Keira by the wrists. Shocked, Keira dropped her weapon and looked into the old woman's hazel eyes.

* * *

The pulsating lights disappeared leaving behind a solid, blue waltz of light, moving in waves to the music like a reflection of the ocean.

"How did she look?" Colby demanded again.

Mikey shook her head and turned on her heel.

"No, wait," Colby pleaded, catching her by the arm. "I didn't mean to…"

"Don't worry, your good guy status is still in tact," she said. "You've been straight up with me the whole time. I understand that we came as friends, nothing more. I just thought it would be more yahoo and less boo hoo."

"You're right," Colby said. "Sorry I ruined the Ball. I guess I at least owe you a dance."

"Yeah, you do."

He nodded to the dance floor, but something in his blue eyes made her hesitate.

"What's wrong?" he asked.

"Wanna know what she looked like? She looked mad. Real mad."

"Oh."

"No, no," a knowing smile pressed on her lips and she cocked an eyebrow. "She looked *passionately* mad."

* * *

Keira woke up with a start on the rooftop. She wiped drool from her shirt collar. The kris still lay neatly on her lap. A half-empty cup tilted in her hand. She sniffed at it, wondering what kind of spirits would cause such strange dreams.

Soon she realized that the music had stopped. Kids filtered out of the gymnasium. She watched Jumper twirl Ann down the steps. Colby's car was already gone. Brun was right. Valley View High was safe for another night.

Chapter 13: My, What Big Teeth You Have

Like thunder, the rumbling grew louder and louder until it reached Ann and Keira. The girls squealed and stomped their feet along with the other fans in an ocean of red and white.

Ann could barely contain herself. Jump's final home game had proved to be an exciting one. Keira loosened up a bit too.

It was about time, Ann thought.

Keira's home life certainly wasn't stress-free these days. Arden now joined August on daily trips to the other side of the barrier. "Something about translating an old book…more sit 'n' wait research," Keira would say.

They would usually rise early and return late. She had barely seen either one of them in weeks.

Keira missed them, but she wasn't the only one. Without them, Bianca grew more and more anxious with each passing day. Her mind was on Arden's warning about the Harvest. She didn't bother to hide her fear from Keira, who shouldered it alone.

Ann had to get her out of the house, if only for a little while. This distraction was her idea. A football game, Senior Night to be exact, was the perfect way to unleash some of the tension that burdened her friend.

"I need to head down to the fifty yard line to get a few pics for the paper," Ann said. "Come with?"

She actually had her own press pass and everything. Keira saw her flash it at the front gate when they came in.

"Nah, I'll stay here and watch our seats," Keira replied. "Have fun."

"I'll be right back," Ann promised just before melding into the crowd of students and parents heading to the field for the Senior Night half-time procession.

Keira stood up to stretch her legs. Her body wasn't meant for sitting so long.

It was a chilly night. Fortunately, she had opted for her heavy jacket and toboggan. Even in her warn cowboy boots, her feet kept warm and cozy in wool socks. She slipped her hands into her pockets and gladly discovered her gloves.

"Let's blow this jock jamboree!"

Keira shrieked. "Mikey, you scared the crap out of me. Where did you come from?"

Mikayla Collins climbed over the seat in her multi-layered black skirt and landed beside Keira. She shoved a half-eaten, mustard-heavy hotdog in Keira's face. "Hold this."

"What are you wearing? You look like you're going to an audition at a Halloween-themed strip club."

"That's exactly what I was going for," she beamed sarcastically, the effect exaggerated with extra blinks of her gold–tipped eyelashes. Her eyes under them shone as black as her hair which was twisted up in wild knots and braids all over her head.

Keira usually liked Mikey's bolder fashion choices. That was not the case this time. Her current outfit seemed to be the result of a blind reach into the dryer.

Mikey met Keira's skeptical eyes, "Don't give me that look. I have school spirit. I *am* wearing school colors like everyone else."

And it was the twisted truth. Under a furry, cropped jacket, she wore a blouse, a deep-plunging halter thing made of some sort of liquid-looking material in a vivid shade of Valley View Viking red.

Keira looked her over to get the full picture. The top seeped into the waistline of a flouncy, layered black skirt. A thin strip of bare skin was visible between the bottom of her skirt and the top of her over-the-knee leather boots.

"Take a picture. It'll last longer," Mikey mumbled as she stuffed the remaining hotdog into her mouth. It disappeared in one bite and the werewolf girl moaned happily.

"Not to distract you from over-enjoying your hotdog, but that's Ann's seat. She's going to be back in a minute."

"Oh, I'm not staying. I was serious about blowing this off. I've got something to show you."

"I'm not going anywhere," Keira said.

"Have it your way," Mikey shrugged. "Just thought that you'd want to see what Broo's up to."

"Uhg," Keira grumbled. "How long's this gonna take?"

"I'll have you back in a jiffy. Travelin' Ann will never know you were missing."

"Fine. Lead the way."

Mikey stretched her long legs over the bleachers. She made her way over to the stadium steps and slid down the handrail to the bottom. She was tapping her foot impatiently when Keira finally stepped down.

"You're wasting precious time, prophecy mouse."

"Cool it. Someone will hear you," Keira warned.

"And they'll think I'm talking nonsense. Just look at me."

Keira thought that she was probably right. No one would take Mikey seriously in that getup. Then on second thought, obviously there was someone who might like it. He did, after all, ask her to the dance.

"Where's Colby?" Keira finally brought herself to ask as they exited the front gates.

Mikey stopped and scrunched up her nose.

"How should I know?"

Her jaw set, Mikey stepped back into her long stride without waiting for an answer.

Keira trailed the werewolf girl, her attention floating back to the stadium and Ann who was probably at that moment watching Jumper and Pastor Johnson walk across the field with the other parents and senior football players, cheerleaders, and members of the band. Ann may have said that she was there for the newspaper, but she was really there for him. Just as she always would be.

And from Ann and Jumper, her thoughts turned to Colby, wondering if he was hurt by Mikey's complete dismissal. And for a moment, just a moment, she even felt bad about for him.

It was a quick moment.

Mikey practically floated as she strode away from the school. She was more poised than Keira had ever seen her before. Typically, Mikey loped everywhere she went. An easy, cool dripped from her. Tonight the werewolf girl was standing tall, confident…regal.

Keira pulled her dagger from her boot as silently and quickly as a mouse twitches an ear, but it was too late. First it was a prick. Then, ice stretched from that spot and spread through her veins. She dropped her dagger and batted at the dart in her neck. Her hands slowed despite her desperation. She barely moved them back in front of her in time to catch the ground.

"Broo?" Keira breathed. It was hard to push the syllable out as a curtain of black tickled the edges of her vision.

"Do you realize that this should have been my night?" Broo shrieked and it seemed not unlike a temper tantrum. "I would have been in my cheerleading uniform in my rightful place as captain. The guys would be falling over themselves to catch a glance at me. The girls would be wishing they were me."

Keira's hand flinched and Broo, still looking like Mikey, stopped momentarily to kick Keira's dagger out of reach.

"But no. You couldn't leave things be. Now, I have responsibilities and you've turned everyone against me."

Keira tried to say something, but it came out little

more than a breath. She could no longer feel her arms. Her toes prickled lightly.

"Everything was just fine until you stepped out of hiding and into my life. I could have rode this high school thing out, then maybe college, but NO. You had to reveal yourself and escalate my timeline to the throne," she sneered. "If I have to do this Harvest thing, then you are going to be the main..."

Broo's voice faded to a constant, low hum as Keira finally fell into unconsciousness.

* * *

Keira was roused by a choking black smoke. The wind blew it relentlessly against her hot cheeks. She coughed, but soon realized she couldn't bring her hands to cover her mouth. They were bound tightly behind her back.

She rolled to escape the billows and immediately felt cool relief on her face. The grass held a sweet, wet dew; a sharp contrast to the heat of the bonfire at her back.

The wind shifted taking the terrible smoke with it. She opened her eyes wider and concentrated on seeing through the night. Her eyes struggled to adjust, but there was one thing she could make out through the blur; the glowing light of the full moon high in the sky. The full moon was good sign. It could only mean one thing…somehow, she was still on the human side of the barrier.

Lit ashes glided down like burning snowflakes. The bonfire raged in the center of the clearing surrounded by woods. Keira rubbed her hands against her ropes, but they didn't budge. She started to roll again. If she could get to the trees, perhaps she could hide, get a few moments to get her bearings and figure things out.

It took only another half rotation before her arms jerked back. She was at the end of her leash.

"Wouldn't have believed it if I didn't see it," she heard Broo's distinct voice snap. "Rolling away, just like the story about her mom. Guess running away 'runs' in the family."

She could tell that the Empress was close. Keira positioned her left leg to give its full support to a rounding kick with her right. To her shock and delight, it connected.

The Empress toppled over with a very non-royal sound. Keira quickly rebounded, shoved the heel of her cowboy boot on the metal stake that tethered her to the ground, and gave it a swift kick. Then another. And another. The turf opened up around the stake, sure to give way completely with a fourth strike, but before that could happen, Broo slid onto her and grabbed her throat with mogdoc-formed claws.

Broo leaned in close and whispered, "This is all happening because of you."

She wrenched Keira up then loosened her grip slightly. It was just enough so that Keira could take a shallow breath that held with dread in her throat.

Broo had shifted back into her human form. Her hair unbound with soft curls looked to be a bright gold against the black sweater and pants that she wore. Keira noted that she was dressed more like a warrior and less like royalty.

Keira frantically eyed the area around them. After all, warriors typically don't fight alone. She saw no one. That's what she thought at first. Then something fluctuated, just at the lowest edge of her vision.

The forest floor was black and moved like water. All around, shadows writhed and undulated in mass.

"What's happening?" Keira gasped.

"Welcome to the Harvest," Broo explained in a close whisper, reciting the next part as if it were a class assignment. "Therefore, in the shortened days before winter's first kiss, the mogdoc ruler calls upon the shadows of the human world to scour the Earth and bring forth its bounty."

Broo pointed out to the waves of black shadows hovering over the grasses before them. "Those naughty little things, they seep onto the sleeping and weak, the unsuspecting humans. And once their victim's air is cut off and their consciousness lost, they will drag their victims across the forest floor to me. We're having a party, a grand celebration with more blood than a mogdoc can stand, and when I, the first Empress of the Empire, have had my fill, it is the tradition set by my father that I will bring the other bodies across the barrier to feed my people." She bit her lip wanly. "I will command the Harvest, then no one will dare challenge my rule."

"You don't want to do this."

"I am not weak," Broo glared. "The Harvest is my duty. I sacrificed my humanity the day I accepted the crown. I refuse to bend under the burden of the choices I have made."

"You can't."

"That, little mouse, may be more right than you know," Broo lowered her voice a bit and squished up her nose. "They're not exactly cooperating."

"Who?"

The Empress's long blonde curls bounced as she

stood. She had Keira's full attention as she raised her perfectly moisturized human-looking hands. Those hands moved as if to conduct a symphony, cutting the air gracefully in perfect rhythm to an unheard, ancient music.

The shadows moved slowly at first, little more than a vibration. A low hum settled over them.

Keeping her movements precise, Broo increased the speed with which her hands moved. Her gestures became more grand, reaching higher. The shadows responded with the changes, building into a writhing current. The sound they made filled the meadow.

Broo pushed forward with both hands, and in the language of her mogdoc forefathers, commanded them to rise. The shadows bubbled up, rose high, and just as quickly dissipated into their previous low-flowing hum.

"Oh pooh," Broo kicked the ground. "See what I mean? You have to fix this."

"I'm not helping you collect bodies to feed mogdocs."

Broo rolled her eyes.

"You are so tragic," she said. Displeasure clearly displayed in her pout. "You think you actually matter. Honey, here's a tip, bait shouldn't talk."

Broo turned her back on Keira and toward the bonfire to warm her hands. Keira wedged her foot on the stake again. Her boot slipped off the top. The Empress had used her tremendous strength to drive it into the earth. Only an inch or two remained above ground.

"And don't get any ideas about going mouse on me," Broo said with her back still turned. "The shadows may collect humans for me, but they keep the smaller creatures for themselves and they're really…really…hungry."

Chapter 14: Reaping the Harvest

Keira tugged at her bindings. They held tight. She scoured the ground around her; a rock, a stick, anything that could be used to weaken the ropes. Why wasn't it like the movies? There was always something useful within arm's reach in the movies.

Yards away, the shadows writhed on the ground; holding for instruction. Waves of black rode up and down as if anchored to the ground. They were like her, Keira thought; eager to move forward, but bound to wait and watch until orders came.

Keira tried again to loosen the buried stake. The smooth soles of her boots slipped off again and again. There would need to be more above ground for her to get an adequate grip.

"Don't give up. The top of the stake is jagged. Maybe you can use it to cut through your ropes. Get closer and rub them against it," she heard a voice call out.

And her heart sank.

"Colby, where are you?"

"Up here."

She looked up. Only the full moon looked back.

"Where?"

"Back here."

She followed the sound of his voice to a large oak, not ten feet away. Its wide base was blackened and gnarled. Branches snaked out like sharpened tentacles in every direction with the exception of two. Those two branches held close to the trunk and behind them the two boys dangled. Shadows reached up for the smaller one, licking the bottom of Drew's feet. As he kicked at them, leaves and bits of bark fell toward the ground, but were swallowed up by the black.

"The stake," Colby urged again. "Use it to cut your ropes. Hurry."

Fire, fueled by guilt, burned inside her and she kicked again. The stake still didn't budge.

She hauled herself up to a sitting position. The wind blew her hair back. Only it wasn't the wind, it was the Empress suddenly upon her.

Orange embers fell down her face, forcing Keira to close her eyes. Heat seared her forehead. Colby was screaming. Drew was screaming. Broo was laughing.

Keira fell onto her back. Broo's laughter echoed in her head, swelling it with rage. She blindly rebounded by thrusting her feet into the air.

"Easy." Brun caught her legs and gently placed them back on the ground. "You don't need her for the Harvest," she heard him say. He wasn't talking to her, but to his sister, the Empress Broo Gammen.

"No, but I apparently need you," she said. "Give the shadows the order, and I will let her go."

"Like I told you before, no," he answered, lowering to undo the ropes at Keira's wrists.

Her slap shattered the night like thunder. Keira looked to Brun's face. Red flamed across his right cheek. His green, mogdoc eyes flared as he turned on his sister.

The siblings moved with inhuman speed. Keira tried to track their movement.

First, Brun rolled onto Broo, pinning her to the ground. She brought up her feet as her shoulders hit the ground, and as she landed, shoved out a kick so hard that it threw Brun back five feet.

Broo became a blur as she rushed at her brother. Brun landed on his knees, and paused only long enough to look up. His arm swung heavily in a wide circle, catching Broo around the neck. Her back slammed into the ground. Another hard kick brought Broo heels over her head and back to her feet.

Not to be deterred, she came at him again. They swirled into a blur. Shoves, kicks, and punches placed with expert precision took them across the grass of the meadow. The two bodies moved with incredible speed and force.

Twice Keira glimpsed the red of Broo's blouse, but other than that, the fight was impossible to track with human, or even guardian, eyes. The motion ended with Broo's back slamming against Colby and Drew's tree. Brun breathed hard over her.

This was only a moment's respite. A high branch cracked and came crashing to the ground. They flashed over it, and Broo shoved Brun onto one of the sharp branches.

Its point broke through Brun's shirt. His face twisted in pain. The blue of the material turned to dark purple at his shoulder. Blood seeped through the fabric; spreading out too quickly like a flower blossoming on time-lapse video.

Keira started to kick the stake again, but at the last moment swung her feet the opposite way, into the air, as hard as she could. The stake jerked loose from the ground and over her head.

The girl scrambled to it and with hands still bound, flung it at the mogdoc Empress. Broo caught it in mid-air, her lips pulled back in a fierce grin.

Broo bowed deeply, pulling the zippers from above her knees to her ankles. The leather boots came off with a slight kick.

It was cold, much too cold, for bare feet on the forest floor, but the Empress was not bothered by it. In another flash of movement, she was in the oak tree.

Holding the stake at Colby's head, she screamed, "Do it, Brun! If you refuse, I will kill him and she will never forgive you. Do it now!"

Keira's hair lifted in the rush of air that accompanied Brun's arrival at her side. He had pulled himself from the branch. He looked past his bloodied shoulder to Keira.

"Do it now!" the Empress screeched again.

Brun searched Keira's face for guidance. He found none. Her chest heaved; her eyes locked on the Hayes boys. "Stop! No!" she was screaming.

"Look at me," Broo ordered her brother, her voice an impatient shrill. "I *will* do this. You know that I will."

The branch holding Colby against the tree felt tighter against his chest even though it hadn't moved. The sharp point of Broo's metal stake stung; wedged against his skull.

Drew wailed, and the others screamed at one another. However, to Colby, their sounds seemed distant. He was focused on one thing…eight moments in time.

He put a hand on top of Broo's as she held the stake. "He can't order the shadows either. I've seen him try and fail. You've fought and deceived to the point where the shadows can no longer identify a mogdoc ruler. So, the shadows have chosen a new master."

"How could you know that?" Brun stepped forward.

Brun's words were as good as a confirmation. Yet, the Empress knew her brother wouldn't give up anything more.

"Who?" Broo pulled the stake back and leaned down so that her lips brushed Colby's forehead.

"Kill me," Colby whispered. "If that's what it will take. Kill me. You're not getting what you want."

"No harm will come to her. You have my word. Just say the name. Please, Colby."

In that instant, he knew that Broo believed him. *No harm to HER,* Colby thought. In his mind, he analyzed the Empress's words. Broo had not only believed him. She had already come to a conclusion on the identity of the shadows' new master.

Colby turned his head to the side to catch sight of the Empress. Her head was jutted forward staring at Brun and, by his side, Keira. Reckoning dawned on the boy.

In a way, it all made sense…the child of sun and moon, a mystical anomaly, just like the shadows themselves.

"Broo," Colby whispered, not sure he had ever

actually called her by that name before. The sound of it must have shocked her too. He felt the shiver that rolled through her body.

"End this," he said. "We can all walk away right now."

She was already shaking her head before he finished.

"It's too late. The Harvest is my only hope. I need this," she whispered and it wasn't the Empress talking, but the girl he once knew, the girl he once dated.

A tear rushed down her cheek. "Give me the name and you save my life."

"Let them go," he pleaded. "I will stay with you and we'll work this out. Please."

"The name…" her lips trembled.

He held her eyes in his.

Colby Hayes was not the kind of boy that kept secrets.

A responsible guy, he never put off homework. He gladly did his chores. He always ate his vegetables. He never told lies.

"It's me," he lied.

His eyes reflected like the ocean back at Broo. Colby closed them slowly, hoping against all hope that his dishonesty was enough.

Broo sucked in a small breath. Her lips came to Colby's cheek.

"Thank you," she whispered. Her kiss lingered lightly on his cheekbone, then to his temple where the stake had touched his skin.

Brun's eyes rushed to Keira. A chilling breeze picked up, but she didn't seem to notice. Her sights were set on Broo.

Keira's mouth came open slightly. Her breaths came ragged. Her forehead wrinkled. She couldn't look away, though she knew she would later wish she had.

Broo slid down the wide trunk. Her bare feet touched the ground without a sound.

Brun stiffened as she approached. Keira still bound at the wrists stood at his side.

"Take your mouse home, brother," the Empress said. "Our business is done."

"You're letting us walk away? What did he say to you?"

Broo's hand lifted gracefully into the air, nails extended, she etched a line into the thin air before her. Silver light seeped from it.

"Go. My window of generosity is closing."

"No!" Keira yelled through clenched teeth. She shook violently as she spoke. "No! Not without them!"

"You may take the kid," Broo said, the repulsion plastered on her face. From behind the branches that held him captive, Colby nodded as if to say it was okay.

It did little to convince Keira. She screamed and thrashed as Brun put his arms around her and stepped toward the mogdoc threshold.

A foot away, he stopped. He shook her shoulders. "Keira, focus," he whispered; his eyes deep and pleading on hers. He pulled a thread and the bindings around her wrists fell to the ground.

Brun flinched, though something about it was unnatural. Keira saw it on his face a second before it happened. The flinch was premeditated.

He put a hand to where the tree branch had

punctured his shoulder. Blood smeared across his fingers. His expression changed. His brow settled low on his forehead, making him look both tired and defeated.

"What are you doing?" Keira asked. It was like watching an actor prep for a dramatic scene. Brun didn't answer. When he was ready, he turned to Broo, blocking her view of Keira.

"Let him go, and I'll help you. I have a little power over them."

He lifted his hand weakly and the shadows swarmed to him, pulled up into the air, then just as quickly dissipated. "If both of us try together."

She didn't trust him or his implied solution. That truth was plain on her face. The tricks of manipulation he used were part of her arsenal too: Displays of weakness can be used to lower defenses.

She kept a keen eye on him as she spoke a few sacred words that allowed the branches of the tree to unfurl. They eased Colby and Drew to the ground behind her. She heard the grass crunch under their shoes, but she didn't turn around.

"Brother, if there is a coup in the empire, the Sect will not leave a Gammen alive," Broo warned. "This is the only way to restore respect to my reign."

"I know," Brun agreed grimly. Dread closed his eyes.

"Take your love and her charge. Go! I can't waste any more time."

Broo's chin lifted. There was a change in the air, an uneasy stillness. She heard something. The sound steadied into a low hum like a vacuum cleaner switched on.

She whirled on the spot where she stood. A wall

of shadows had risen up and now towered over her in a crushing wave. The boy, Drew, stood with his little arms raised over this head, clearly in control of the shadows as they plummeted to the earth with exceeding force.

Colby swiped Drew aside, but the wordless order was already given. Colby turned, looked back to Broo. Keira shielded her eyes from the light that came off him. His feet hit the ground as the world plunged into slow motion…his steps too small, too slow…an outstretched hand…the pounding in his chest…the rushing sound of the shadows…a pull that wasn't enough…and finally, a flash of brave resignation, the same that graced the little girl's face as her father seeded the Atlantis token in her arm.

The shadows settled on the ground for a moment, a moment of silence, before parting ways, leaving the Empress lay crumpled on the ground.

Keira rushed to Drew's side. She scooped him up, his face wet from sobbing.

"Home," Drew whimpered into her shoulder.

She spun, looking for Colby. Her eyes found him on the ground. Bruises covered his hands as they held his face in them.

He looked to Keira and dared to ask, "Is she…?"

Keira didn't know. She hadn't checked. Her only thought was of Drew and Colby. She looked to Broo now. Brun was standing over his sister's too-still body.

"Is she dead?" Colby repeated this time pushing the word out. His voice trembled as he scrambled toward the sunken ground where she lay.

Brun put a hand up which stopped Colby short. "No, let me."

They watched as Brun silently drew a new threshold in the air. He put his arms beneath Broo and brought her up to his chest. Her head lolled back, revealing purple and black skin down her neck and beyond. Her clothing was mere shreds. Lines of blood trickled from her mouth. Her legs dangled over his other arm, bobbing with his movements, not of their own accord.

Brun's eyes raked over them. For a moment, he looked as if he wanted to say something, but instead he turned and carried his sister through the threshold and disappeared.

Chapter 15: Convergence

In the days that followed there was quiet. No kidnapped friends, no mysterious intruders, and best of all, no impending doom.

It was like a vacation. Well, no, it *was* a vacation; Christmas break to be exact. However, the festivities of the holidays did little to alleviate the quiet, but instead helped it to grow stronger and deeper.

The friends, one-by-one, decided to spend time with their respective families, apart from the group. Even Arden took a few days of vacation. He packed his bags and headed across the barrier to meet up with siblings in Elsted.

When Ann received Jumper's call, she was glad for it. It was New Year's Eve, and he suggested that they spend the evening at a local amusement park. They had fallen into a routine of late. He would come to her house to watch movies; or she would go to his house to play video games. It had been a long while since they had an actual date, so she welcomed the idea.

His Jeep pulled up to the house around eight. She was out the door before he even came to a full stop. He met her halfway up the sidewalk.

"Hey," he said.

"Hey," she smiled back.

He cleaned up good, maybe a little too good. He was wearing jeans, but his usual long-sleeved tee or jersey was gone, replaced by a button-down dress shirt and jacket. Brown shoes peeked beneath his jeans instead of his usual cross-trainers.

"Aren't we going to River Canyon?" Ann asked suspiciously.

"Yeah," he said with a turn around to show off his new ensemble. "I just thought it might be nice to step it up a little."

When he was through with his model's twirl, he dramatically thrust an arm out to escort her to his vehicle. He opened the passenger side door and helped her inside.

And when they reached the park, he opened the door again for her. His hand held hers, to assist her out and down to the ground. After she stepped away, he closed the door and picked up her hand. His lips met her knuckles.

"Charmed," she laughed.

He let out a small chuckle. He then presented his arm to her again and said, "Shall we?"

"We shall," she said and leaned her head against his strong arm as they made their way to the front gates.

Once they reached the entrance, Ann patted her pockets, but there was no need. Jumper already had her pass in his hand with his and was waving them both in the air. The attendant nodded them through, and as soon as they emerged from the gate, Jumper took off.

They ran together, hand in hand, her following closely behind him.

"Where are we going?" she would ask, but he didn't reply.

When they rounded the train station, she tried to stop to catch her breath.

"Just a little farther," he smiled.

She smiled back and nodded and they were off again, winding around the pathways of the park toward the sound of fireworks she couldn't yet see.

Finally, they came to a grand Roman arch that separated the park's award-winning rose gardens from the roller coasters and rides. Jumper slowed.

Ann giggled, she couldn't help it. He was whisking her away to be alone and it struck her as quite romantic. Perhaps they would kiss at midnight under the clock tower in the mock Italian square, or maybe he had planned a romantic dinner at the Scottish pub outside the Loch Ness ride.

Jumper stopped as her mind fluttered with the possibilities. He folded his arms so that she came closer, and just about the moment she was ready for a kiss, he lifted his brows and moved ahead. Their hands still linked, she had no choice but to follow.

The garden was beautifully lit in the cool, winter evening. Giant white lanterns hung from arbors. Topiaries and shrubs were adorned with tiny, twinkling white lights.

She spotted Keira in a far corner just as a will-o'-the-wisp took off from the guardian's hand. Dozens of the wisps weaved through the air. Their dancing flight added the perfect amount of magic to the night. The wildly quixotic scene before Ann took her breath away.

Jumper was continuing to move, but he had slowed down considerably. He lifted a thick, red velvet rope that cordoned off the area.

"After you," he said.

She hesitated.

They could go around. It probably wouldn't take too long to get back on track. Ann was sure that they weren't supposed to be in there. She was about to tell him as much, but then she saw Colby standing at the first crossroads on the closed path.

Ann looked to Jumper. He gave her nothing.

"What are you…" Ann started to ask, but Colby pulled Jumper from her.

"Everything ready, bro?" she heard Jumper ask.

Colby nodded shortly.

"Unexpected," she heard him say, "…arriving for the last half hour."

He seemed worried, but whatever it was, it only seemed to humor Jumper. He patted Colby on the back. "I got this," he assured his buddy.

Ann eyed Jumper carefully.

"It's time," he erupted. Only his grin was as big as his eyes.

He took her hand again, and she followed him down the right path. When she turned to look, Colby waved, but stayed in the same spot.

"Jump, what's this all about? Isn't Colby coming too? I saw Keira back there too. Where are we going?"

"Right here," he said, bringing them to an abrupt halt.

The path before them opened up to a fountain. The wisps zipped in and out of the water, leaving a trail of sparkling icy droplets in the air. The water flowing from the fountain's center reached a high crescendo with the music that flowed through that area of the garden.

"It's beautiful," Ann breathed, her cheeks a little rosy from the run.

"You're beautiful," he said, sliding a hand across her cheek and meeting her lips with a soft kiss. "And how I became so blessed to be a part of your life, I'll never know," he exhaled.

She kissed him once more before he could take off again. His eyes lingered shut even after their lips pulled apart.

Jumper took Ann's hand and held it over his heart. He touched his forehead to hers and said, "I will never love anyone as much as I love you. And I will never be loved as deeply as you love me. When I doubted you, you saw past that and you always knew my true heart. Always. And I…"

"Hew," he stepped back and shook out his limbs. "This is a little harder than I thought. I didn't expect an audience. Remind me to thank you later."

Curious, she looked past him. Her eyes widened.

There among the bushes and topiaries, on the adjoining paths and between classic faux marble statues, were dozens of women, all watching the couple. All with dark red hair, though some contained bits of gray. All with knowing brown eyes, though some shining with tears. All the same height, though varying ages. All of them were Ann.

And the gravity of the moment fell upon this Ann, the Ann of the present. Her heart raced and the air she unconsciously took into her lungs came fast and shallow. She almost didn't hear Jumper's next words.

"It wasn't long ago that I nearly drowned. It made me realize that a life without you is one that I don't want to live. Ann Clara Martin, I give you all that I am, and I promise to love you now and for all time. Will you," he said, taking in a gulp of air as he lowered to one knee. "Will you marry me?"

"Yes!" she screamed and jumped into his arms. He rose to his feet, still clutching her tightly, and swung her around.

"Wahooo! She said 'Yes'!" he yelled to the throng of watching Anns.

He pumped his fist in the air. The crowd laughed and cheered, except one. Dressed in all black, she had been pushed from the group, told to leave, told she shouldn't be there.

Jumper put Ann back on her feet and pulled a box from his jacket. His hands were shaking as badly as hers as he slipped the ring on her finger.

His eyes wouldn't leave hers, nor would hers leave his. Though they were surrounded, it was just the two of them. Time felt as though it stood still (though it really didn't). Then they kissed, and it was as tentative and full of hope as their first kiss.

Again and again they kissed and laughed and laughed and kissed, each time more loving than the last. They kissed as the others popped back to their appropriate times, sounding off like fireworks which faded into the night.

When the last had gone and the kisses began to

dwindle, Ann's mind started to race. Jumper wrapped his fingers around hers as she counted off the tasks to be done.

"We'll need a date, and a place, and we'll have to choose the wedding party, and order the invitations."

"I was thinking we would wait until after graduation if that's okay. Don't want anyone thinking I knocked you up," he teased.

Ann ran a finger through her love's hair. "You're right. We have a lifetime together. And there's something I have to do first."

Chapter 16: A Step Back

Ann stood at Keira's front door ready to knock. Her fist just held in the air. To this point, she had traveled to her own past less than a handful of times, but she had never before interacted with anyone.

I*'m not changing anything, just a nudge in the right direction*, she told herself.

Surely that wasn't enough to break the rules. She was nervous, and she had a right to be. Technically, a noose is a loophole too.

So Ann was taking her time. It wasn't her idea to be here. It was Keira's.

On the night of the shadows rising, Colby had intervened. He had tried to save the Empress.

Saving a life was something any decent person would do. It's what anyone would expect from Colby.

However, his sympathy for Broo, his willingness

to stay with her, troubled Keira more than she would admit. He would have stayed behind with Broo if Drew hadn't sent the shadows against her.

That was the kind of guy he was…brave, kind, compassionate, loyal to his friends. And Broo, she had been a friend to him once, a very good friend.

Ann hadn't been there that night as she should have. She owed Keira this. She owed Colby this. They needed to protect Colby from himself.

The Keira of this time wasn't going anywhere. Ann remembered the extent of her friend's injuries on this day. It was early summer, just after their freshman year. Keira had been bedridden for several weeks after facing off with the Emperor.

Ann took a breath of the warm May air. Keira's house looked the same: same brick, same door, same porch, same porch light that stayed on even in the daytime.

Then the door opened.

"Annie Martin, come in, come in. No use lingering on the porch," Nana said with a welcoming smile.

Ann almost shed a tear at the sudden sight of the old woman. Of all the things she had prepared herself for, this was not one of them. It had been three years since she saw Nana last. In her world, Nana was on the lam, a fugitive in the eyes of the guardian council. She couldn't help herself. She wrapped her arms around Keira's first protector.

"Oh, thank you, sweetheart. You don't know how much I needed that."

"You've been worrying about Keira?"

"That child is luckier than a leprechaun with a rabbit's foot on Sunday."

Ann laughed. She wanted to stay with her for a while, but that's not why she was there.

"Is she awake?" Ann asked.

"She's been in and out, but you can wait in her room with Colby if you want. I'll be in the kitchen if you need me."

"Thank you," Ann said as she started to move down the hall.

"And dear," she heard Nana call behind her. "Just a nudge. Nothing more."

Ann stood stunned as the old woman trailed off without a look back.

"Yes, ma'am," she uttered, although Nana was already too far away to hear it. With that, she turned back to the task at hand. *Focus*, she told herself as she lengthened her stride down the lonely hallway.

Ann welcomed curiosity like an old friend. On that day, it led her to Arden's room. She couldn't help but peek inside.

At that point in time, he hadn't arrived yet. It was still Nana's bedroom. Lace doilies graced the furniture tops and photos of rose vases graced the walls. The familiar white vanity sat in a dark corner. The room seemed much larger when it wasn't filled to the brim with stacks upon stacks of Arden's history books.

Not wanting to have to explain why she had wandered into Nana's room, she decided to move across the hall. When she popped her head in, she saw Colby sitting in a chair pulled to Keira's bedside. His nose was buried in a book, while Keira lay fast asleep.

Ann moved toward the bed, and he looked up.

"Hey. Where's Jumper?" he whispered.

She gulped unintentionally and hoped he didn't notice. "He might be here later. Um, can we talk outside for a minute?"

He nodded and she was relieved. Keira may only be pretending to be asleep. She wouldn't put it past her friend and what she had to say, Keira couldn't hear.

Colby rose from his station and followed her to the kitchen and then out the back door. Nana was doing dishes in the kitchen sink and looked up briefly as they passed, finally choosing to continue her work.

She led Colby across the backyard. It had just been mowed and the scent of fresh cut grass mixed with the summer sun and filled her lungs. She savored it and stayed silent as she brought him to the old maple tree in the far corner. Ann had good memories of the tree. She and Keira had spent many summers dangling from its branches.

She fell into the wooden swing connected to its limbs. This was different in her present too. Over the last three years the ropes had frayed. The seat was carried away by an intense storm a few weeks ago, or maybe months ago, it was hard to know for sure.

All these things from the past were too distracting. So much so, that they were causing her to ignore Colby and that only fed his uncertainty. She could tell from his body language that he was raising his shields, putting his guard up. He wouldn't sit, instead choosing to stand against the tree.

Where would she start? Like every good reporter, she chose to start at the beginning.

"Fifteen years ago, a very special baby was born of sun and moon."

"Right," Colby interrupted. "I already understand. You've all got super powers. Do we really need to talk about this right now? I shouldn't leave

Keira alone…"

He doesn't even realize how important he is in all this, she thought.

Ann forced a smile. "You better listen. I don't have much time."

He was so young, so impatient. He made a big gesture out of moving from the tree to sit on the grass, like a little kid who was not getting his way. She ignored his behavior and continued.

"Okay, of sun and moon…anyway… there are many who believed that this baby would grow to become a great warrior and overcome the Mogdoc Empire."

"And this baby is you?"

"No, but many believe it is Keira. So, as a baby, she was hidden among humans where she could be educated and trained in safety, until it was time. Her parents gave her up to conceal her identity. Since they couldn't be with her, they provided her with many protectors. I only know three of them."

Of course she was lying, but thought that it was best to keep the number low. She needed to remain mindful of divulging too much future information.

"I don't know if Keira even knows who all of them are. Nana, of course, is her primary trainer and protection. Two travelers, my parents, also pledged to protect her, but now their pledge has fallen to my sister and me."

"Katie's only ten years old."

The image of Katie at ten distracted her briefly. She was sweet back then.

"That's not the point."

"Well, I guess it's good to know that you're watching out for her. It makes me feel so much better that she has someone besides a little old lady to protect her. You know, like a real defender with special abilities."

"That's only part of what I need to tell you. There's more," she continued. "Keira has a duty to perform to bring about the end of Broo, er Brooke, well, the whole mogdoc empire."

She paused a moment to gauge his reaction. She wasn't sure if he would recognize her real name yet. He didn't even flinch. Maybe he knew her by both names.

"Colby, these creatures are so cruel. If you only knew the pain and inhumanity that they've caused."

She couldn't help but think of what they had done and what they were going to do. The numbness started to take over, but she choked it back. She had to in order to succeed with her self-imposed mission.

"Their wickedness is so unrelenting that it also affects the human world, manifesting in the worst kind of evil. Keira must fulfill the master plan at all costs."

"Yes, I know, it's her destiny."

His apathetic response made her blood boil.

"No, Colby, there is no such thing as destiny. This is her calling. I don't mean to sound too corny, but she is the hope of all generations. When she succeeds, she will save both our worlds. So, listen to me carefully. If you try to stop her, I'll have no choice but to stop *you*."

"Why would I stop her?"

"Colby, just listen to what I'm telling you. Keira and her mission come first, before any connection that we have. My whole world depends on it. This isn't going to be easy and she will have to make some tough choices."

And you won't like most of them, she thought.

"Why would I stop her?" he repeated.

"Just see that you don't. I must trust that you will listen to me and never forget this conversation," Ann said as she planted her feet back on the ground. She started to leave, but realized that she had left one loose end.

"And Colby, one more thing," she said in a voice barely above a whisper. She could practically see that imaginary line of time traveler unwritten law. "I'm going to stop by to visit Keira in about an hour. I won't remember this conversation, so please don't mention it."

She raised her arm to him, showing off the battle scar she received on prom night her junior year.

He didn't register it right away. He started babbling on, "Why won't you..."

He stopped midsentence and began to study her body. She saw his eyes flash over her longer hair and clothing. She tried to hide the engagement ring, but suspected that he caught sight of that too.

"You're not the Ann from my time, are you?"

She twisted her lips in consideration of her answer. Finally, she decided that maybe it was best left unsaid. It was better if she didn't give him too much. He could come to his own conclusions.

As she walked away, she caught a glimpse of Nana through the kitchen window. She remembered Colby's earlier words. She repeated them in her head, *someone besides a little old lady to protect her*. She could give him another nudge, nothing that could change anything, just a tiny bit of information that would help in the long run.

"And, Colby, just a word of advice," she said

turning back to him. “Don’t underestimate Nana. She’s no grandmother and is as sly as they come.”

She left him with that. It was a little satisfying to see him confounded. He was just a little too smart for his own good.

She started out of the backyard fence, but in the last moment decided to take one last look at Keira before traveling back to the future. She slipped back into her room. It had remained virtually unchanged over the years. Keira was still sleeping peacefully.

Ann was feeling a bit of that peace too. She felt good. She was strong and in control. This was how it was supposed to be. It was exactly the way that her mother told her it would be on that night several years ago when she first learned that she was a traveler. She surveyed the damage done to Keira’s body by the mogdocs. That was just the beginning of it. They had both suffered much. Keira was born into it, but Ann was drafted. As Ann looked upon her injured friend, she pondered which was better.

“Get your rest now,” Ann whispered. “You’re gonna need it later. We both will.”

For a few stolen moments, she fantasized about taking time to rest beside her friend, but there was still work to do. The mogdocs were quiet for now, but it wouldn’t last. It never did.

Hopefully what she had done today was enough to push things in the right direction without consequences. She took a deep breath as she faded back to the future with a sonic boom.

Chapter 17: House of Gammen

The late Emperor was not prone to giving his children advice. However, he managed to spare a few gems over the years. On the night of the shadows' rising, Brun remembered his father's words as if they were being whispered in his ear.

"Behind every poor circumstance is a great passion for change. Wield it, as it is stronger than any sword."

Just as Ann had predicted, the mogdocs would not remain quiet for long. A flame of hatred reignited and blazed throughout the Empire the night Brun Gammen carried his sister home.

Crowds packed the marketplace as they usually did at that hour. Torches posted along the Citadel walls lit his arrival under the forever flawless black night. Brun stepped from the threshold with Broo in his arms.

Shocked cries and whimpers erupted at the sight of the Empress, her body not lifeless, but battered and broken, beaten to unconsciousness. Smeared blood and massive bruises covered every inch of her body under shreds of what used to be her clothing. A frail hand fell from where he had placed it respectfully on her chest.

Her eyes were closed like a sleeping doll. Her lips slightly parted.

Then right before the hundreds of eyes that packed the marketplace, Broo's body defending itself, began to shift into its natural mogdoc form. Deep purple bruises morphed into broken and bleeding scales. Large gashes appeared on her torso, legs, and arms. Her skin tone took on a sickly gray, rather than its normal, oceanic blue-green.

Only Brun's voice broke past the horrified screeches of the populace.

"Witness, brave warriors, what our enemies have done to our Empress," Brun spoke.

The crowd shushed to bated breaths and murmurs. The eyes of the entire marketplace fixated on the siblings.

Brun's shoulders raised, he seemed formidable at his full height, towering above the mogdocs. Dark blood from his shoulder stained his clothing; his face brandished fresh, bleeding scratches and bruises.

The onlookers couldn't know that it was the Empress herself that caused his injuries. To his audience, he looked as if he just stepped out of a warzone. Brun's presence, though human in form, demanded their attention.

The royal guards rushed him. He growled and his

eyes flashed a threatening green. They stepped back, falling to their knees before him…

"I am the master of the House of Gammen, the *true* Emperor, the Moon of Atlantis, and I will not stand for such insolence, not from magical mice or the mere humans they protect. They think us weak and indifferent, while they grow fat and injudicious. Your fallen Empress was lulled into their foolish notions and empty promises for peace. Look what they did to her. Look! No more," he said, his jaw clenched in a hard line. "No more. By the full power of the Empire, we will hold down our enemies in our merciless grip, take what we want, and watch them with pleasure as they die. Soon comes the day when all will quiver at the mere mention of our name. For we are Mogdoc!"

BONUS

Even the best crafted plans, sometimes fall awry. Remember when the gang had to split up during their rescue mission in the Mogdoc Citadel? While Brun was helping Keira escape from the water well tunnel, Jumper and Colby happened upon their own adventure in Atlantis.

Siren's Call

A Midnight Guardian Short Story

The mogdoc guards were adequately distracted, leaving the Citadel gates wide open for Keira, Katie, Ann and Arden.

Jumper Johnson breathed a sigh of relief. His part in the rescue mission was done. He offered the old man a hand up. A knowing grin slid across his face though he tried his best to hide it.

The two toddled together down the alley, leaving all the street-side booths behind. Soon not even the torchlight of the marketplace reached them.

Jumper fumbled to find his pockets, forgetting the robe covering them. The old man looked to him. The man knew exactly what Jumper was looking for. He pulled a phone from his waist and lit the path before them.

"Thanks, bro," Jumper whispered.

"Shhhh."

"You worry too much. No one can hear us."

"Not yet, shhhh," he repeated and continued down the path furthering them from the Citadel.

Jumper shrugged and rolled his eyes before snatching the phone from the man's hands. He flipped through the screens. "Dude, you have nothin' good loaded."

Jumper looked up from the phone, and pushed a smirk to the side of his face.

The man stopped. He sighed and removed his hood and bald cap. It wasn’t an old man at all, but rather Colby in disguise. It was all part of the rescue mission.

"Jump, I just want to make sure we're safe before letting down our disguises. You heard Arden."

Jumper rolled his shoulders, flicked his red hair back on the sides, and summoned his best impression of Arden. "Blimey, if ye get taken by the mogdocs, you'll be nuttin' but bangers and mash to 'em."

"Wow," Colby shook his head. “That so does *not* sound like Arden.”

"Pirate. British Tooth Fairy. I figure they're pretty much the same," Jumper shrugged.

Colby smiled, "Sure they are."

"You worry too much, bro. No one's gonna know you."

"Doesn't matter now, this is the rendezvous spot."

Jumper stretched his arms over his head. "So what do we do now?"

"We sit and wait."

"Wait if you want, man. It's not every day that I

end up in Atlantis. I'm exploring," Jumper declared, tossing the phone back to Colby.

He caught it just before a rustling in the alley stole their attention. Wordlessly, Colby picked up a wooden pole propped up against a nearby awning. He took a couple of careful steps as he motioned for Jumper to take the opposite side.

The boys peered down the alley. Suddenly, a door opened up behind Colby. Arms reached around him and pulled him inside.

Jumper's strides reached the door just as it shut. He tried the handle. Locked. He stepped back and peered at the sign over the awning. Dangling precariously on a half-rotted peg. It said,

Employees Only
SIREN'S CALL TAVERN

Jumper beat on the door with his fists. To his great surprise, it opened sharply, nearly knocking him off his feet.

He saw voluminous, sparkling pink hair long before a face was visible. The young woman kept both hands on the door, opening it just enough so that her petite frame was all that Jumper could see inside.

Her shimmering periwinkle dress was tight enough that it could have been painted on her body; although paint may have covered up more than the dress did. Tiny crystals spiraled in intricate patterns on her alabaster right shoulder, reaching all the way up her neck and ending at her pink cheek. Eyes so dark that there seemed to be no irises stared beneath silvered eyelashes and took Jumper in from head to toe.

Jumper started, "Uh, good evening…um, ma'am?"

"Umm hmm. Doll, no one's called me ma'am for centuries. This is the employee entrance. Patrons enter from the other side."

She started to close the door, but Jumper wedged his booted foot between it and the jamb.

"Yeah, so, I'm looking for my friend. Have you seen him? Skinny, young guy?"

"Vampire?"

"Not that I know of," he replied with a slight snicker. "Is that what you are?"

"Sugar, do I look like I bite?"

His eyes grew two sizes as her lips pulled into a wide grin over multiple rows of teeth, a hundred thin points, all looked sharp as needles.

"Mmmm," she said with a seductive drawl. "I guess that I do. Not a blood sucker, though."

She reached out to touch Jumper, but he took a step back. The woman eyed him playfully.

"Ya know what? I think I did see your 'friend'. Tall, blond with ocean blue eyes, right? The girls," she purred, "The girls are callin' him Captain Heartbreak. Sweet boy like that makes even this ancient heart flutter a bit."

Her lips pouted. Jumper tried not to laugh.

"Isn't that him?"

He followed the woman's pointing finger to his own chest. Jumper looked incredulous. He lifted his brow and curiously turned around. There standing behind him was Colby.

As he stood staring at Colby in disbelief, the door slammed shut. The two boys were again alone in the alley behind the tavern.

Colby's eyes lazily blinked. Marks left behind by glossy pink and red lips littered his face.

"Dude," Jumper laughed. "What happened to you?"

"Pretty sparkly girls," he whispered dreamily.

"Are you drunk?" Jumper laughed.

Colby didn't answer. In fact, he didn't seem to know that Jumper was talking. He didn't even seem to know that Jumper existed. His eyes drifted over the building behind Jumper. His body swayed to music that wasn't playing. A goofy grin was plastered across his face.

"Sober up, man. I can't take you back like this," Jumper patted his friend's back.

He latched onto Colby's tunic and pulled him down the alley. The boy's legs like Jello; his feet awkwardly hit the path a strange angles.

They moved along the alley swiftly until Jumper spotted a water spigot behind one of the buildings and stopped.

"Sit," Jumper ordered.

Colby fell on his butt.

Jumper turned the wheel on the top of the spigot, collected the water in his hands, and dumped it on Colby's head.

Only it wasn't water.

"I smell like fishhhhh," Colby slurred over the words and ended the phrase with a snort followed by uncontrolled giggling.

"Ewww," Jumper looked at his hands. "Mogdoc fish goo spigot? Seriously?"

He would have continued complaining, but out of nowhere, something fell on Jumper's head. His chin hit his chest. The thing, whatever it was, was still on his head…and it moved.

Though he couldn't see it, he swatted at the beast. It hissed. His feet stumbled across the alley. Colby whooped and cheered; now on his feet and dancing around the excitement.

Finally, Jumper got hold of the creature by the scruff of the neck and held it out. Its smooth black fur glistened in the torchlight. He turned it around to face him.

The cat blinked its yellow diamond-shaped eyes. Well, not really a cat. A skinny, forked tongue snaked from its mouth and reached out more than a foot to flick Jumper's nose.

He dropped the creature, which landed on its feet. Colby clapped his hands and pulled a stunned Jumper by the arm.

"Go! Go! Go! Go! Go!" Colby whaled.

Jumper eased his eyes up. Along the low rooftops and eaves, dozens of yellow eyes peered back.

The boys scrambled away. Jumper felt a tug. Claws dug into his robe and started to paw their way up his back.

Jumper and Colby cut into another alley. Two this time pounced on Jumper. One landed on his left arm. He swiped at it, but it wrapped its body around his arm and held tight. The other slipped from his shoulder. Its claws caught on the bottom edge of the white Unionist robe that he had been wearing as his disguise. The cat dragged behind him as he ran.

The end of the alley was nearing, their path lay in two directions. The left led to more alleyways. The right seemed to open up to the marketplace.

Jumper cut right, pushing against Colby's shoulder. He looked up. One of the cat creatures clung to Colby's head like a fur cap. Another pair, maybe three, pounced onto Jumper.

As they rounded the corner, wearing and dragging more than a half dozen cat-beasts, the buildings separated. Crowds packed the marketplace. At first no one noticed, but that didn't last long. The crowds moved aside. Whispers, laughs, and pointed fingers followed them.

The boys continued to run. The unrelenting creatures hissed and clawed at their clothing. Their tails flicked in the night air.

Jumper looked from side to side. Surrounded, yet no help was in sight. Humans were on short supply on this side of the barrier. Supernaturals, at least those living near the Citadel or trading in the marketplace, weren't the friendly sort, certainly not the kind to offer assistance to those in need.

Then Colby saw it; sparkling and blue like the siren's painted-on dress.

The boys brought their feet off the ground, and the two plunged into the public fountain. The cat creatures screeched and scurried away.

Jumper sat up and rubbed his fish-scented hands over his face. Colby came up with a gasp. He took the air into his lungs as if he had almost drowned in the two-feet of water. He choked a bit before settling on his knees beside his friend.

"We never speak of this again," Colby said.

"Whatever you say, Captain Heartbreak."

SNEAK PEEK

Read on for an exclusive Sneak Peek at Midnight Guardian #5, *Book of the Lost*, coming Spring 2013.

Arden Wright could barely keep up with August's long strides. It was necessity. Minutes were running short and they couldn't be late, or they would miss their chance.

The beam from Arden's flashlight bounced off the tall evergreen trees of the West Woods. With each huff, it moved shakily across the ground, barely offering any help.

August put out an arm to keep Arden from stepping off the cliff's edge. A sprinkling of rocks and clay dirt tumbled. Arden peered over the side, shining his light downward. The bottom lay concealed by fog. There was no telling how deep it ran.

"The Rubrae Cliffs," August spoke. "We're here."

* * *

Over the past weeks, they toted the *Book of the Lost* to wise men, scholars, and even to some of the more unseemly inhabitants of the supernatural community. All told them the same thing. The book was undecipherable. It couldn't be read.

All, until the last one.

Merrick rubbed his hands over the book longingly.

August watched him by the flicker of lantern light in the tavern's back room. Arden stood watch at the door. He leaned against its rustic, wooden frame. Outside he could hear the revelry of the tavern floor, but inside this back room it was deathly quiet.

"Do you know what you have here? All that this tome contains," Merrick purred.

The sound of his voice caused Arden to cringe.

"Careful," August warned Merrick, his fingers tapped the hilt of his sword. "What do you know of it? Can you read it?"

"I just may have information that will help…for a price."

Arden reached into his pack and pulled from it a small bag. He tossed the bag onto the table. It opened up spilling Hershey's Kisses across the surface.

Merrick's eyes sparkled.

Cocao plants did not exist on the banished continent of Atlantis. Chocolate was more rare than gold. He scooped up the spilled contents and pushed them back into the bag greedily.

"The book…" August slammed his sword onto the wooden table.

Merrick replied with a twitch of his pointed ears, "It bears the feather of Ma'at, the Egyptian goddess of balance. I never thought I would see it in all my days, yet here it is in my hands."

"Merrick!" August snapped.

"Ahem. I believe this to be the *Book of the Lost.* I cannot read it, but there are those that can."

Merrick then revealed that only the guardian elders possessed the long-lost knowledge, the secrets of the *Book of the Lost*.

“Surely a guardian as decorated as you would have no trouble convincing them to help,” Merrick sneered. “That is, unless you are hiding this discovery from them. Ehhh, August?”

August lifted his chin to Arden, who tossed him another bag of candy. August this time held it in the air. Merrick’s tongue slipped out of his mouth and across his cracked lips.

“There is more of this for those who value silence,” August said.

“Of course, of course,” Merrick mumbled. “Nice doing business with you, Master Ryan.”

The elf shoved the chocolates into a bag. The noise and candelight of the tavern spilled into the room as Arden opened the door and Merrick scrambled out.

“What are we going to do, August?” Arden worried. “We can’t trust the Council. The Unionists have already swayed them. They’ll just take the book and hide it away.”

“We don’t have to go to the Council,” August said, regret already welling up inside him. “There is another.”

CROSS THE BARRIER

Author & Book News
www.brynabutler.com
www.facebook.com/AuthorBrynaButler

Midnight Guardian Apparel & Gifts
www.cafepress.com/swancrestpublishing

Take the Teams Colby, William, Arden Quizzes
www.goodreads.com

MNN: Mogdoc News Network
Midnight Guardian & YA News
www.twitter.com/mogdocnews

Book Trailers
TheButlerWroteIt Channel on YouTube
YA Trailer Park: www.yatrailerpark.com

COMING Spring 2013
Graduation Day is Coming
Book of the Lost
Midnight Guardian, Book 5

ABOUT THE AUTHOR

After graduating with the honor of Outstanding Communications Student from the University of Rio Grande, Bryna Butler settled down with her high school sweetheart on their family farm along the banks of the Ohio River. She is an accomplished financial public relations and corporate communications professional, that decided to take a detour into the world of fiction.

As for life on the farm, it's never dull; especially with their two young sons who fearlessly provide constant entertainment.

www.ingramcontent.com/pod-product-compliance
Lightning Source LLC
La Vergne TN
LVHW041925090826
845145LV00015B/695

* 9 7 8 0 9 8 5 9 2 7 2 4 0 *